lost in the fractured peaks

CLAIMED BY THE WOLF

LOLA GLASS

Cover Design by Moonpress | www.moonpress.co

To pain and grief
And to new beginnings

one

RORY

I STARED out at the river, wondering if there was a black-market way to receive a new identity. The water moved rapidly, and the heavy grayness in the sky was accompanied by a miserable, chilly drizzle.

The movies made the black market sound so *real*. I'd googled it, but all that had done was make me paranoid the government was going to send someone after me just for looking it up. If it was real, finding it wasn't as simple as searching the internet. Not for me, at least.

My phone buzzed, and I didn't have to look down to know who the text was from, or what it would say.

I looked down anyway.

> **ALLEN**
> Where are you?

Letting out a long, quiet sigh, I closed my eyes.

There had been red flags.

So many red flags.

So *damn* many red flags.

But I'd been lonely, and he'd paid attention to me.

So, I made myself colorblind. The red was green, and I insisted to myself that everything would work out.

I'd been wrong, obviously.

And it had gotten me trapped in an abusive relationship.

I'd tried to leave... and he had chased me.

Repeatedly.

If I tried to leave again, there was a good chance I wouldn't survive it.

My parents and older sister were held captive by their drug addictions, so they wouldn't help me unless I offered them money. And unfortunately, Allen controlled that, too.

I had nothing, and no one.

Even if my google search had brought me to the black market, I wouldn't have been able to pay for the new life I needed.

My phone buzzed again.

And again.

And again.

I fought the urge to throw it into the damn river.

The texts were more of his usual:

ALLEN

Who are you with?

What are you doing?

I'll be there in ten minutes.

Tears welled in my eyes, and I pushed my long, damp, blonde hair off my face.

A woman sat down on the bench beside me, but I didn't look her way. I was so tired of lying about being okay.

"What's your name?" she asked me.

"Rory," I said quietly.

"Pretty. I'm Serae."

If she was asking about my name, she wasn't asking about the bruise on my face, at least.

"You're crying, Rory," the woman added.

My throat swelled.

Dammit, couldn't we stick to the names?

Why did we need to talk at all?

"There's a bruise on your cheek," she added. "I can help you, you know."

My head jerked toward her.

The woman was gorgeous, with white, curly hair, dark skin, and the biggest blue eyes I'd ever seen.

Something about her was… otherworldly.

That was probably just because she'd offered to help me, though.

"How?" My voice edged on desperation. "Nothing has worked.

My phone was vibrating again, but neither of us acknowledged its motion beside me on the bench.

"Give me your hand." She held out her palm.

I didn't know how that would help, but I didn't stop and wonder. My hand was in hers a heartbeat later.

The moment our skin touched, light swelled around us. My lips parted in wonder—or horror—as the light swallowed everything around me for a moment.

The woman's grip on my hand tightened and didn't let go, not that I tried to pull away.

Who was she?

What was she?

Did she have some kind of… magic?

Damn, I hoped so.

The light faded a moment later.

When my vision cleared, my lips parted.

The river in front of me was gone completely, replaced by a wall of rich, black stone with swirling gray streaks. There were deep, winding cracks in the stone, and small plants grew from them at an angle, jutting toward me.

I turned around halfway, and my jaw legitimately fell open when my gaze moved over the horizon.

Mountains—I was in the mountains.

Huge, stone mountains covered in trees with massive black trunks and blood red leaves. Out in front of me, an endless forest of red-leaf trees stretched as far as I could see.

"This isn't Earth," I whispered.

"No, it's not. Welcome to Evare, Rory. The wolves will find you soon."

I looked back at her, and found her eyes glowing brightly. Considering I knew she had magic, the glowing eyes didn't seem like a stretch. "The wolves?"

"Wolf shifters," she clarified.

"*Werewolves*?" My voice was incredulous.

"Like you said, this isn't Earth." She flashed me a smile, though her expression looked... tired. "The wolf shifters need mates to stay alive. I cursed them permanently, on accident. You're here to mate with one of them."

My eyebrows shot upward. "What does that mean?"

"The humans I know call it irreversible arranged marriage. It'll start with a guy biting you."

My eyebrows raised higher. "Irreversible arranged marriage? And *biting* me?"

"Yep." Her smile faded, and her eyes closed for a long moment. "I've got to stop doing this. Only forty-four more to go."

"Forty-four more *what*?"

"Don't worry about it. Just… stay here. The wolves will find you soon," she repeated, and then patted my knee lightly. "The shifters can't hurt their women; it would kill them. You'll be safe here."

With that, she disappeared.

Literally, she just *vanished*.

"What the hell?" I turned around on the bench so I could see the view again, and my knee bumped something.

My phone.

I looked down at it, tense and nervous… but it had stopped vibrating.

My hands trembled a little as I picked it up and tapped the screen.

No service.

I could see Allen's last few texts, but he couldn't send anymore.

And he couldn't track me or find me.

Or hurt me.

Tears stung my eyes again, for an entirely different reason.

I stood up quickly, striding toward a massive cliff off to the side of my bench. My hair blew around my face, still slightly damp from the drizzle back on Earth, but I paid it no attention.

I was *free.*

And I was getting rid of that damn phone.

The toes of my black high-tops dug into the smooth stone as I reached the ledge. There was probably an insane gleam in my eyes, but I didn't care.

I'd embrace the hell out of the insanity if it meant I was safe, or at the very least, free.

I pulled my arm back, and without a moment of hesitation, launched my phone off the cliff.

Allen would never control me again.

No one would ever control me again.

My gaze went back to the bench, my chest rising and falling quickly. Serae had told me to wait for the wolves there. I didn't want to get tangled up in whatever weird *irreversible arranged marriage* they had, but wolves were dangerous. If I tried to run from them, they could probably track me, and it wasn't like I could outrun them.

Vowing to myself that no matter what happened, I would never let a man treat me poorly again, I walked back to the bench.

And I waited.

. . .

THE WAITING WENT on for so long that the suns in the sky—yes, plural, I spotted three—went down, and two moons went up.

Two moons.

Three suns.

Definitely not on Earth anymore, which made me smile.

My growling stomach did *not* make me smile, however.

I was getting too hungry to remain on the bench, and without knowing when the supposed werewolves would show up, I didn't really want to risk staying where I was.

So, I finally got up and made my way back to the cliff I'd thrown my phone from. It was getting colder by the hour, so I was glad I had on a comfortable sweatshirt, and had pulled the hood over my head to keep my ears and neck warm. If I'd known I'd be out in the cold, I would've worn an extra pair of leggings, but I hadn't known.

I eyed the cliff's drop-off with a grimace.

There was no chance I'd survive that fall.

Shuffling along the edge of it, I looked for a smaller drop.

No dice.

I heaved a sigh and walked back to my bench, plopping down with a grimace.

Guess I was back to waiting.

. . .

I DOZED on and off through the night, until a howl in the distance woke me.

Jerking awake, I turned my chest to the bench's back and peered out at the forest below me.

I couldn't see anything, but I'd heard a howl. That had to be a wolf, didn't it?

A few minutes passed.

Long, long minutes.

Finally, I heard something scratching against stone, and scrambled over to the ledge.

My eyes widened when I saw a man below me, scaling the cliff without any visible gear. His gaze lifted upward, and his glowing, golden eyes froze me in place.

When he pulled his gaze from mine, he started climbing faster.

I walked backward slowly until I hit the stone. I had barely seen the man, but those golden eyes were creepy.

What was I going to do if he tried to hurt me? I was short and skinny, and I'd never been able to protect myself from Allen before. Serae said werewolves couldn't hurt women, but why should I trust her? She had abandoned me.

Fear clenched in my abdomen as the man's head cleared the ledge of the cliff, followed by the rest of him.

My eyes widened in horror as he stood in front of me.

He was completely naked, glowing the same gold as his eyes, and huge *everywhere*.

His light skin was absolutely covered in black and gray tattoos, and the muscles on him were outrageously large. His shaggy black curls would've been considered attractive by most women, but I no longer allowed myself to be attracted to dangerous men.

Or any men, really.

Or any women, for that matter.

Love and attraction were clearly not compatible with me.

Especially as they applied to a man who could kill me with his bare hands, without breaking a sweat.

A soft whimper escaped me when his eyes caught mine.

He looked me up and down slowly, then gave a terrifying rumble, and prowled toward me.

"Don't hurt me," I whispered. "Please, don't hurt me."

He covered the distance between us, and then stopped just a breath in front of me. He was at least a foot and a half taller than my 5'0", so I didn't think he'd even need to *hurt* me. He could just squash me like a bug.

My chest rose and fell rapidly as he reached for me, and I squeezed my eyes shut against the fear.

Instead of causing me pain, his fingers caught the hood of my sweatshirt, and pushed it away from my face.

Then, his palms landed lightly on my shoulders.

So much more lightly than I expected.

A savage snarl escaped him, and I tensed in response.

But he only demanded, "Who hurt you?"

Who...

What?

I couldn't stop myself from peeking my eyes open just a little.

"Who touched you, female? They left bruises on your skin," he nearly roared.

He was very near to yelling at me, but for some reason, my fear was fading away.

Maybe because he was angry that I'd been hurt.

That was a green flag, right?

Or was I being color-blind again?

Gah, I didn't know.

His hands cupped my cheeks, the gold in his eyes having faded just a little. Despite the shock of his touch, having his hands on my skin sort of... relaxed me. "Who?"

"My fiancé," I whispered. "Allen."

"Tell me where to find him so I can end his life," the man commanded.

It was probably a bad thing to admit, but my heart melted just slightly at his words. "He's on Earth. I don't know how you'd find him."

"I will find a way."

"It's okay. You don't have to. I... I think I might be safer now."

His eyes flared brighter gold. "You are *mine*, female. I will protect you with my life, until the day we cross the veil together."

My own eyes widened.

What was I supposed to say to that?

What did it even mean?

"Okay," I said, my voice trembling a bit.

"I must bite you, to claim you. The pain will be temporary, and the magic will heal you rapidly."

Serae had mentioned the biting.

I tried to shrink back anyway. "Please, don't hurt me."

"I have no choice." His fingertips brushed my chin gently, shocking me and freezing me in place.

A heartbeat later, his teeth found the place my neck met my shoulders.

I cried out as the sharp pain cut through me, but instead of pushing the man away, my hands wrapped around his thick arms.

He released my shoulder almost immediately, and his tongue dragged over the wound. He was right; the pain ended quickly.

His gaze lifted to mine, and I watched the golden glow fade from his eyes, leaving them a deep black color that somehow still glowed slightly, like Serae's had.

"I'm sorry," he said, his voice low and gravelly.

"It's okay," I whispered. Somehow, I meant it. "Do you have food? And water? And shelter of some kind? I'd like to get off this cliff if I can."

"Of course. You'll need to hold on to me while I get us down."

He was going to climb down the cliff.

Of course he was.

I nodded and he turned, lifting me onto his back with hands far gentler than I was acquainted with. My arms went around his neck. "Hold on tightly. What's your name?"

"Rory."

"Rory, I am Amarok. I'll take you back to my pack, and never let another male touch your skin."

My eyes widened. "Okay, then."

Really, what else was I supposed to say to that?

I had seen the rage of a possessive man, and my body had taken the brunt of it. If werewolves were possessive, I would have to find a way out of whatever our mating was.

There wasn't a chance in hell I would go through that again. Not if there was anything I could do to stop it.

But for the moment, Amarok was my best chance at surviving and figuring out the world I was in.

So, when he started climbing down, I held on for dear life.

RORY

WHEN WE REACHED the bottom of the cliff, Amarok continued carrying me piggy-back style until we found a small, fresh-smelling creek and a tree dotted in some kind of fuzzy black berries. They didn't look appealing, but food was food.

I drank from the creek when he told me to drink, and ate the berries without complaint. They were surprisingly delicious, and I had a lot more of them than I initially planned.

"Okay, I'm full," I told Amarok, after rinsing my hands in the creek and drinking a little more water. "How far is your pack?"

"It's a five-day run. Two days through the Fractured Peaks, and three in the Broken Woods. We can stop halfway and spend the night with another pack to shower and eat, if you'd prefer. You'll ride on my back while I run in my wolf form, but it will be more tiring than you expect."

If I *preferred*?

Damn, life in Evare was already so much different than life on Earth. I hadn't been allowed to have opinions in years.

I hesitated to answer.

My initial reaction was to tell him he could choose, but...

Did I have a preference?

"What will the other pack be like? And what's your pack like?" I asked the questions quickly, not wanting to give him time to change his mind.

"My pack is small and quiet, but there are five other women from your world there. There are two mated couples, but everyone else is unmated. The pack we would be visiting is loud and boisterous, full of those who have been mated for a long, long time."

"And mated is like married?" I asked.

"Yes," Amarok confirmed, his gaze lingering on my face.

It took me a minute to work through my feelings.

I didn't love loud and boisterous, but after a few days of running, I *would* probably want a shower.

And if I had to stay with a pack permanently, I was glad it was the quieter one. Having other women from Earth there too would be good, probably. I wasn't great at making friends, but maybe I could learn. Or relearn, I supposed.

At twenty-three, I should've been in my social prime, shouldn't I?

I guess I didn't really know.

But Allen had slowly convinced me to drop all of my friends, so it didn't particularly matter. I would figure it out, if just to spite him.

"And you and me are considered... mated?" I asked carefully.

"Halfway mated. To seal our bond, you would need to bite me as well." He gestured to his neck. "There's no rush. We'll have an eclipse in a few weeks, and our bond will break then, but we will restart it afterward if you're willing."

Oh.

Well, that didn't sound so bad at all.

I'd be tied to Amarok for a few weeks, and then I'd be... free?

Shit, the idea was unreal.

I wouldn't even know what to do with myself, especially in a new world.

"What if I'm not willing?" I asked, wrapping my arms around my middle. Though logically he hadn't given me a reason to think he'd attack me, some part of me still believed it might happen.

His lips curved upward, just the tiniest bit. I couldn't help but feel a little attraction to him when I saw his smile, but ignored it thoroughly. "Then I'll sit outside your den until I've convinced you to."

My throat swelled. "Like a jailer?"

His smile vanished. "Of course not. You'd be free to live your life, Rory—but we're fated. To me, that means we vowed to stay together in a life before this one. You were mine, and I was yours. I will do whatever it takes to prove my worthiness to you."

The lump in my throat didn't budge, and I had no idea how to reply. So, I just nodded.

He was definitely possessive.

Definitely controlling, too.

There wasn't a chance in hell I could let myself feel anything more than the mild attraction I currently felt for Amarok.

At least he had warned me—even if he didn't realize that was what he'd done.

"It would be good to stop and shower," I added, when I realized I hadn't really said what I preferred. "Can we stop for just the night with the loud pack so we can shower? Without making friends or anything?"

"Of course." He dipped his head. "Ready to start moving?"

No.

I was nowhere near ready to get going.

But there wasn't another option, was there?

So, I forced a tiny smile. "Yes."

He didn't look convinced, but didn't call me on the lie. "I can speak into your mind because of our bond, so don't be scared when you hear me in your head."

I blinked.

That was unexpected.

He shifted forms smoothly, and my eyes widened at the sight of him.

The wolf was massive. Absolutely, insanely massive. His head was level with mine, and his fur was the darkest shade of black I had ever seen. He would blend into the shadows, especially among the black trunks of the trees around us. He was still glowing gold, thankfully, so he couldn't hide from me.

He could eat me for dinner if he decided to.

And I was supposed to ride on his back?

Shit.

Someone should've warned me. Someone other than Serae, because she was absolutely terrible at warnings.

"Don't be alarmed," his smooth voice said into my mind.

My heart nearly jumped out of my chest, so yeah, *not being alarmed* wasn't an option.

"How do I get on your back?" I asked him, ignoring my pounding heart.

He sat down on the ground, his belly against the smooth stone of the mountains he had called the Fractured Peaks.

That made climbing on easy.

I slipped a leg over his back, sitting down near his neck and leaning closer without touching him.

"Hold on to me, Rory. I don't want you falling and hurting yourself when we move," he warned.

Right.

He was going to run.

Touching was inevitable.

I tensed for discomfort, and carefully slipped my hands into his fur.

It was... soft.

Really soft.

And the warmth of his body beneath the fur actually felt pretty heavenly.

I had come to despise Allen's touch so much, I'd started to wonder if I'd ever enjoy physical contact again. But touching Amarok wasn't so bad when he was in his wolf form. And his hands hadn't felt bad on my face, either.

Not that I was going to think about that moment again.

"Are you ready?" he asked me.

"Yes," I lied again.

Once again, he didn't call me on my lie.

Instead, he started walking.

I had expected him to break out in a run, so it was nice to get the feel of his movement like that first. The rhythmic motion was relaxing, and I didn't mind at all when he slowly picked up speed, until we were flying through the Peaks.

The wind dragged my hair out behind me, and my body pressed tighter to Amarok's back as the initial fear faded.

His warmth soaked into my skin as black and red trees flew past us at ridiculous speeds, and I couldn't help it—my lips stretched in a smile, and then in a massive grin.

Freedom.

That was what freedom felt like.

Despite the wildness of being in a new world and the fear still curling somewhere within me, I was free.

And that was *everything*.

WE RAN through the rest of the night, and continued running as the suns began rising in the sky. Amarok finally stopped on an outcropping of the mountain we'd just crested, right beside another stream.

He shifted back, and I ignored his nudity surprisingly well. We drank water and ate another kind of strange fruit, then watched the suns rise in silence for a few minutes. The sky was a mixture of vibrant, molten colors, and I couldn't help but be in awe at the beauty of it.

Something told me Amarok had stopped there just so I could see it.

Or maybe just so *we* could see it.

I didn't want to consider the implications of either option, so I didn't ask, and he didn't offer the information.

When he shifted back and sat on the ground again, I climbed on his back wordlessly. He took off into the trees, and we fell into the rhythmic movement that I was coming to love.

EXHAUSTION WAS CREEPING in by the time we stopped for lunch, and when the suns began setting, I was having a hard time keeping my eyes open. I kept dozing off then jerking awake, and couldn't seem to stop myself.

The suns were still setting when Amarok stopped near another creek—or another place along the same creek— where we could look out at more of the mountains and trees like we had in the morning.

"It's still light out," I murmured to him, as I slipped off his back.

I managed all of two steps before I stumbled.

A pair of thick, huge hands caught me by the hips, and my body flushed at the contact. His grip was firm, but gentle, too.

He was being careful with me.

Not treating me like I was breakable, but treating me like I was... important.

My throat swelled again at the care he was showing me.

Was that a green flag?

It felt like a green flag.

But before, everything that had felt green had really been red, so I wasn't sure.

"You need to rest. We'll stay here for the night." His voice wasn't hard, but it wasn't soft, either.

That wasn't up for debate.

"The last thing I want is for you to fall off my back while we're running, Rory," he added.

"It's fine. You don't need to explain it to me." I went to pull his hands off my hips, carefully, and he released me before I even had to touch him.

That was new, too.

"Of course I do. You deserve to know the reasoning behind what we're doing and where we're going." There was a bit of growl to his voice that made my body warmer.

"Thank you." I didn't want to let myself think about the potential flag-color of that comment, so I walked over to the creek and kneeled down, cupping water and bringing it to my lips again.

Amarok joined me, and we drank silently. He picked more of the fruit we'd had for lunch, showing me how to identify the tree it grew on in case I was ever alone in the forest. I seriously hoped that would never happen, but it seemed smart to know anyway.

Then we sat down and ate, falling into more of the earlier silence.

My mind was on the sleeping arrangements, which neither of us had brought up yet.

We waited until we were done eating, and then Amarok cleared his throat.

I closed my eyes for a long moment before looking over at him.

"It gets cold at night, this high in the Peaks. If you would prefer to sleep alone, I understand completely, but if you need warmth, I am more than willing to share mine. I'll be sleeping in my wolf form, as well, so there would be less discomfort.

Damn.

Green flag?

Red flag?

I had no idea.

Really, I just needed to stop thinking about flags.

"Let's just try sleeping alone and we'll see how we do," I said, giving him a small smile.

"Of course."

The suns were nearly gone, and darkness was quickly engulfing us, so I went ahead and curled up on the stone. I was so tired, I was sure I'd fall asleep almost instantly.

As expected, I was sleeping peacefully a few minutes later, with plenty of distance between me and the wolf.

three

RORY

MY SLEEP LASTED all of two or three hours.

Then, I was awake and shivering in the dark creepiness of night in the Peaks. There were millions of stars over our heads—and no visible moons, strangely enough. There were a bunch of what looked like large fireflies flying around us, which helped me see a little.

The wolf was right; it was freezing cold. I hadn't noticed while we were running the night before, because I was pressed up against him and he was so damn warm. I should've remembered the chill I'd felt while sitting on my bench on that cliff, though.

I tried to tough it out, but after twenty minutes of violent shivering, I finally croaked, "Are you awake?"

He didn't hesitate before answering in my mind. *"Yes."*

"Can I lay next to you?"

He answered by crossing the distance I'd left between us and laying on his belly beside me.

I rolled onto my side and draped an arm and leg over his massive back. A groan escaped me at the incredible warmth of his body, and I buried my face in his fur too.

The glow around him grew brighter, but I didn't ask why.

Something told me I didn't want to know about the glow.

"Thank you so much," I mumbled into his fur.

"Thank you for allowing me to provide you warmth," he murmured, and I felt the brush of his furry face against the back of my head. He wrapped himself around me as much as he could, and the warmth slowly began to soak into my fingers and toes.

"What happened to the moons?" I asked him, surprising myself by starting a conversation. It would take time for me to warm up all the way, and honestly, I was curious.

"What do you mean?"

"There were two of them last night, and now I can't see any."

"Do the moons on Earth not rotate?"

"Rotate? We only have one moon, and it's up every night, like clockwork."

"Ah. In Evare, our moons rotate on different timetables. One rises every other night, and the other rises every third night. They only rise together every sixth night."

Damn.

"How does that even work?"

"Magic, I suppose. Everything in Evare functions through magic."

I guessed I couldn't argue with that.

"Do all three suns always rise?"

"Yes, every day. They usually stay in their own portions of the sky, as well. Once every three months, they all overlap, and we call it an eclipse. The day of the eclipse is intense for all, and every being past the age of maturity is overcome by the heat of lust and desire."

Well, that made me flush.

"What's the age of maturity?"

"It's different for all species. For shifters, it's seventeen."

I was hoping he'd say thirty or fifty, but no luck.

"Should I ask why you're glowing?" I asked, finally almost entirely warm.

"At this point, probably not."

I decided to take his word on it.

"Okay. Goodnight, then." I whispered.

"Goodnight, Rory. Sleep well."

Murmuring a *"you too,"* I drifted back to sleep, blissfully warm.

. . .

WHEN WE WOKE up the next morning, I felt much more at ease around Amarok than before. The sleep had helped. The conversation had, too.

We were still quiet as we ate and then started running, but not *as* quiet.

And while we ran, I asked a few questions.

He gave me all the information I wanted, and more.

I learned that Evare was full of magical beings, and that there were dragons, fae, elves, demons, gargoyles, and many others. They all had their own mating processes and rituals, and their own parts of the world.

He told me why the werewolves needed mates from Earth—because Serae had cursed the wolf shifters to only have male children, assuming she could undo it, and then failed.

The shifters had been dying out ever since because of some kind of insanity that came with immortality, called *immis*. Immis could drive them mad if they weren't mated, and there were only fifty surviving unmated wolf shifters because of that. All of them were in his pack.

He explained that mated pairs were more like friends or partners than lovers. That sex was involved much of the time, but not always. That fate sometimes decided two people just needed to be tied together as friends.

That last bit of information relaxed me, unlike everything else I learned.

When I ran out of questions, he asked one of his own.

He asked me if I would tell him about Allen.

My fingers clenched in his fur, and I told him no.

He accepted my answer, and didn't push me for anything more.

I was still uncertain about the flag colors in our situation for the most part, but I knew that one was green. Allen never would've accepted a no to a question like that.

IT WAS LATE that night when we finally reached the pack we'd been looking for. The trees had changed as we approached, looking more like the ones on Earth, with brown and black trunks and green leaves.

There were some people out and about despite the late hour, talking and laughing and sharing food. None of them tried to stop us, though I noticed many, many grins when they saw us.

I couldn't help but lean a little tighter against his back when I noticed their grins.

"They'll give us space," Amarok assured me, as we continued moving through the pack's city in the mountains. *"They're aware of Serae's lack of control as to where our humans land when she transports them in. Our packs both have scouts scattered through every part of the Woods now."*

I stayed quiet, knowing the werewolves we passed would hear me if I spoke up so close to them.

"One of my packmates had already caught your scent and was running toward you when I passed him, lost to my mate run. He would've brought you to safety soon enough, even if we hadn't been fated."

I wasn't sure whether to be relieved someone else had been coming for me, or bothered that Amarok had gotten to me first when the other guy may not have bitten me. He really hadn't done anything to deserve my dislike though, so I decided I wasn't going to be angry with him.

We were both doing our best in a new situation, it seemed.

Soon enough, we reached a large tree. Amarok warned me to lean in as we reached it, and I gripped his fur tighter as I bent down like he asked.

He soared through a low hole in the tree's trunk, then stopped long enough to push a large lever. It slid a massive rock into place, closing the door behind us completely.

That probably should've worried me, but strangely, I trusted Amarok enough that it didn't.

He jumped downward, and my heart flew into my throat at the sudden drop. Of course, he landed so smoothly I barely felt the impact.

"The huvim—the lightbugs you saw outside—can't get in with the den closed, so it'll be a little dark for you. I think we'll both sleep better knowing no one can get in, though."

He was right.

I didn't completely trust Amarok, but I *really* didn't trust any of the other werewolves. Even the other humans from my world would be difficult to trust, because I didn't know how long they'd been in Evare or why they'd ended up there.

My eyes adjusted to the darkness of the den much better than I expected them to. I could see the outlines of a bed, a bathroom, and what may have been a kitchen. None of it looked exactly the same as what we had on Earth, but it was close enough that I didn't have to wonder what it was.

Amarok sat down, and I slipped off his back quietly. My feet ached from wearing my high-tops for so long, and my entire body felt crusted with sweat and dirt. There really wasn't dirt in the Peaks, but for whatever reason, I still felt dirty.

"The shower is in here." Amarok strode across the room, just as naked as always. I forced my eyes to stay on the back of his head, not wanting the image of his undoubtedly-perfect ass imprinted in my mind. "There are spare clothes in the closet. If you're comfortable with it, I can wash your current clothing while you sleep, and you can spend the night in the spare clothes."

Oh, that was tempting.

I forced myself to stay cautious, though. What if the spares were lingerie or something?

"Can I see the clothes?"

"Of course." He gestured me to a door near the bathroom, and I tentatively followed him in.

I still couldn't see perfectly, but I could see well enough to identify a bunch of oversized t-shirts, and a few outfits that looked like bodysuits. There was another section in the closet with huge shorts, pants, and more shirts.

"Shifter women usually wear these beneath these." He gestured to the bodysuits, followed by the huge t-shirts.

There would be no pants... but I guess I couldn't blame them for that. Who really liked wearing pants?

"Okay, that'll work. Thank you." I carefully picked up the strange hangers holding a bodysuit and oversized shirt. "I can wash my own clothes, though. There's a sink, right?"

"Of course. I would be privileged to wash them, but if you prefer to do it yourself, I understand."

My cheeks flushed. "Alright."

What else was I supposed to say to that?

Geez, the man was just too much sometimes. I didn't know how to respond to someone offering to take care of me, or my things.

"Take as much time as you want," he told me as I stepped into the bathroom. His glowing eyes lingered on my face, and I nodded.

"Thank you."

His lips curved up in a small but genuine smile. "It's my pleasure, Rory."

I closed and locked the door, then leaned up against it lightly, squeezing my eyes shut.

Helping me was his *pleasure*?

What kind of world had I ended up in, exactly?

I FIGURED out how to turn on the shower without too much of a hassle, despite the dark, then stripped and stepped beneath the water. The heat felt so nice, I barely managed to bite back my groan.

Bliss.

It was absolute bliss.

Then again, pretty much everything about the past two days had been bliss. There was some natural shock to finding myself dragged into a new world, but the joy of being free from Allen was so immense, it outweighed that shock. And the feeling of freedom that accompanied riding on Amarok's back while he ran was honestly just indescribable. I still hadn't gotten tired of it, and doubted I ever would.

I washed my hair with what I decided was the shampoo and conditioner by sniffing. It was too dark to see the texture or color, so I wasn't positive I was correct, but figured it wouldn't hurt anything if I wasn't.

After I scrubbed the rest of my body with what was hopefully normal soap, I stepped out of the water long enough to grab my clothing. My fingers struggled with the fabric as I washed it in the sink, but I didn't miss my washing machine.

I didn't miss anything about Earth, truthfully.

It took some time before I decided they were clean enough, and then I hung them all on the towel hooks in the bathroom, knowing Amarok had no clothes to put up.

After I dried off with a towel, I slipped into the borrowed clothing. The bodysuit was stretchy and ridiculously soft, and felt like a second skin. The oversized shirt wasn't stretchy, but it was light and comfortable. Its bottom hem fell to the middle of my thighs, so I definitely wasn't exposed.

I hadn't expected to feel at ease in the borrowed clothing, but I did. Really, I felt more at ease than I had in years.

I took my time towel-drying my hair, and then after a moment's hesitation, braided it behind my head. Allen had told me my hair looked terrible when it was tied up or back, so I had rarely bothered with it. But it was nice to get the long, thick strands out of my face and off my neck.

Since I wasn't trying to win Amarok over or seduce him or anything, there was no point in trying to look good. It might even work in my benefit if I *did* look terrible.

After I tied the braid with a bit of fabric I found in a drawer, I had no other excuse to stay in the bathroom any longer.

So, I let out a long breath, and then opened the door.

RORY

MY EYEBROWS LIFTED when I found Amarok in the kitchen, wearing soft-looking pants. I had to get fairly close to see him well enough.

"You're cooking," I blurted, before I could stop myself.

He looked over his shoulder. His eyes trailed slowly down my figure, then back up before he growled softly, "Veil, you are *perfect*."

My face flushed.

I had no idea what to do with that compliment. Especially when my hair was braided, and I didn't have on any makeup.

"You're cooking," I repeated, fighting the urge to wrap my arms around my abdomen for the sake of comfort. "Do werewolves cook a lot?"

"A male werewolf is responsible for fulfilling all of his female's needs. It's his privilege to cook for his mate. So, yes. We cook a lot."

They *enjoyed* cooking for their mates?

This world grew more bizarre by the moment.

Allen had lost his shit with me when I didn't have a hot meal waiting for him after a long day of work, even when I'd worked more hours than he had.

"Did you have a career, on Earth?" Amarok asked me, turning back to his food. "I've seen the lists of careers humans have, but I admit, I've spent most of my time patrolling to make sure Serae can't abandon any more females without us finding them quickly."

"I did." I bit my lip, walking carefully over to the table I could see. The darkness made it too difficult to make out the colors of anything, other than Amarok's glow.

He was quiet, and I got the feeling he was hoping I would answer his question about my career.

I was tired, and a little disoriented, but calm. So much calmer than I'd been in so long. When I felt so safe, it was hard to know what I should and shouldn't say. So, I answered him. "I was a nurse. I... my family wasn't good to me. They were addicted to drugs, if you know what that means. I graduated high school early and got a scholarship so I could get away from them sooner. My nursing program was accelerated, too, so I finished a few years ago. But I met Allen a few months after I started my first job, and... yeah."

Worried I'd said too much and not enough at the same time, I bit my lip again, harder.

"Nurses care for your sick?" he asked.

Relief spread through me.

At least he'd understood part of it.

"Mostly. I worked with the women having babies, taking care of them during and after birth."

The look he shot me was intense. "You had a very noble profession, then."

My throat swelled. "I guess."

"Don't guess, Rory. Know. You were a good human."

Tears stung my eyes. "Thank you."

His words were so different than the ones Allen had given me, even in the very beginning of our relationship. I had never been enough for him, in any way. And while I'd been emotionally disconnected from him for over a year, I was still around him, constantly. Being insulted, day after day.

I'd never had someone compliment me like that, and it made me feel so good, I didn't even want to know whether or not it was a red flag or green.

"How long were you…" he trailed off, uncertain how to ask the question.

I knew what he was asking, though.

"With Allen?" I supplied.

"Yes. How long were you with Allen?"

"About three years. The first few months, I thought he was perfect. He paid attention to me, and listened when I talked. Most of the men I'd met didn't do that. He brought me flowers after we had a disagreement, and I thought we'd be together forever. I was so, so stupid." Closing my eyes, I let out a long breath.

I had never told anyone the full story.

I'd called the hotlines before the first time I tried to leave, before I'd known that he had cameras in our house and my phone connected to some kind of recorder. He'd heard everything I'd said… and I'd never been brave enough to talk, since.

That had been a year and a half earlier.

Part of me wanted to tell the story. To get it off my chest, so I could at least attempt to let it go.

But I couldn't let myself open up that completely to Amarok, so I didn't say anything else.

"What did he do to you?" the man's voice was gravelly.

I borrowed a few of his words from when I'd asked about the glowing. "At this point, I don't think you want to know."

His body tensed visibly, but he didn't argue or growl at me.

We were both silent while he finished cooking, but the delicious smells of whatever he was making kept me from growing stressed or worried.

And how bad could he be, if he came from a culture where the men were trained to feed their woman? I wouldn't let myself get attached to him in any sort of a romantic capacity, of course, but still.

He was taking care of me, like he had since we met. That had to count for something.

If I *had* to be mated to one of the men, why not Amarok? He had basically offered to keep our relationship platonic, and I wasn't against platonic. It would be nice to have a genuine friend.

Knowing he wanted to be more than that might ruin it, though...

I wasn't sure.

Maybe I'd decide after we got to his pack.

He made us both massive plates of food, and I barely stopped myself from salivating at the sight and smell. I didn't know what it was, but it smelled good and looked fancy, with a bunch of different components and some kind of a sauce over all of them.

"Thank you," I said, and meant it.

He dipped his head in a nod, though he still looked a little tense.

We both started eating, and holy shit, it was delicious. The foreign flavors melded perfectly, and though I had no words to describe them, they were quite possibly the best things I'd ever tasted.

I was lost to the food until I finally scraped the plate clean. When I lifted my head, I found Amarok watching me closely, his own plate empty and a satisfied gleam in his eyes.

My face warmed. "I've never had a man cook for me before."

The satisfaction in his gaze thickened. "You liked the meal?"

"It was incredible."

"Good." He took my plate, set it on his, then strode back to the kitchen. The tension in his shoulders was gone.

Somehow, watching me eat had relaxed him.

Damn, Evare was bizarre. Or maybe it was just the werewolves.

I realized I was being a terrible guest—if I could be considered a guest—and spoke up quickly. "I can clean the dishes."

"No."

I blinked at his firm refusal.

Definitely hadn't expected that.

"I've been told that it's natural for humans to exchange mundane roles—that if one person cooks a meal, the other cleans up afterward—but I'm not comfortable with it. You're welcome to sit nearby so we can converse, or tuck yourself into bed if you'd prefer, but I feel it's my duty to clean as well."

I blinked again, and again.

What was I supposed to say to that?

He was setting a clear boundary—which was a green flag, I thought.

Probably.

Maybe?

Sigh.

I wasn't sure.

And I wasn't uncomfortable with letting him do the dishes. The whole situation was too strange for that.

Maybe if I'd been a little more comfortable with him, I would've walked over and sat next to him. It seemed like a fair trade; a conversation for a meal.

But I didn't want him to think I saw us as a couple, a team, or anything along those lines. So, I quietly crossed the room, then tucked myself into the bed. The sheets were smooth and silky, though chilly. I shivered a little, but did so silently.

I knew he wouldn't climb into bed with me without asking permission—and doubted he would even ask—so I quietly spread out on the bed. My lips curved upward as I did, because I was *safe*.

There was no more cowering at night, no more clinging to my edge of the bed and hoping Allen would go to sleep silently.

No more pain.

No more abuse.

I had to navigate the strange, arranged marriage situation I'd somehow landed in, but without Allen there, I could do *anything*.

Closing my eyes, I let out a long breath. There was a weight on my chest and shoulders that had just... vanished. It was gone, completely.

And now, I was free.

Free to live, and breathe, and laugh. To feel the sun on my face, and free to smile.

To make friends.

To curl up with a book for as many hours as I wanted, any damn day I decided to.

Hell, I was even free to fall in love, if I wanted to.

Which I didn't.

But... I had always wanted love.

Maybe after I'd figured out how to be myself again, I would consider looking for a partner among the wolves. Maybe Amarok would understand that, and he would be okay with just being my friend until I was ready.

Or maybe he wouldn't, and he would try to win over some other woman.

Honestly, that was okay too.

I needed time to find myself. He would accept that, or I would tell him in no uncertain terms that we would never be together.

My smile widened at the thought.

He wouldn't hurt me.

He *couldn't* hurt me, if Serae was right.

So what was the worst that could happen when I told him no? He'd be a little angry?

I almost laughed.

If anyone could handle a man's anger, it was me. The violence, I couldn't deal with, but the anger?

I could manage that.

Allen had tried to break me, but now that I was free from him, I knew all he'd done was make me strong.

Strong... and slightly afraid.

But I would focus on the strength.

Just to be safe, I wouldn't tell Amarok that I wasn't willing to consider being his mate in any romantic capacity until we were with his pack again. I didn't know the other women, but I hoped they would back me up, and protect me if I needed it.

Not from his violence—I knew he wouldn't be violent with me. Or at least, I was pretty sure. But from his possessiveness, if needed.

I spread my body out a little more completely on the mattress. It was still a little cold, but warm enough that I could relish the chill, because it meant I wasn't sleeping beside Allen any longer.

Amarok finished the dishes and took a shower, and I remained awake until he had shifted to his wolf form and curled up on the floor beside the bed.

He wasn't going to force me to do anything.

The knowledge of that made me feel warm and happy, and I fell asleep cuddled up with my blankets, content in my freedom.

five

RORY

WE SLIPPED OUT of the borrowed den the next morning, after I reluctantly changed back into my cleanish Earth clothes. Then, we were off again. My lips were still stretched in a wide grin as we ran, and my body relaxed further with every hour I spent in Evare, completely and entirely free.

During the next day, I noticed that my hair looked different. The blonde Allen had insisted I needed seemed to be *pinkish*. I thought I was going crazy at first, but resigned to ask Amarok about it when it looked darker by the time we stopped for the night.

"Does my hair look pink to you?" I asked him, as he plucked massive fruit from a tree for us. We'd made it out of the Fractured Peaks and into the Broken Woods, so my back was to a thick, black tree's trunk.

"Yes. My magic has begun changing you," he admitted.

I blinked. "What?"

"The way Serae explains it, humans from your world are magical... sponges."

The way he said *sponges* told me it wasn't a word he used often. I wondered if he'd picked it up from one of the Earth humans, as he'd called them.

"Okay," I said, prodding him to continue.

He handed me a piece of fruit, and waited until I took a bite before going on. "You soak in the magic of whichever beings you are surrounded by or connected to. So, even if our bond breaks, your body will have internalized my magic, and you will be a wolf shifter. It seems to take most of the females a month or two to shift, but in theory, they could do so much sooner."

I blinked again.

And again.

Part of me was scared to death by the thought of transforming into a wolf. Another part of me was thrilled, because it meant I would never be weak or powerless again.

"Alright. And that's why my hair is pink?"

He nodded. "You're in the process of transforming, and female wolf shifters aren't like the males. Our coloring is mist and shadows; yours is bright and alive."

Well, then.

"So you think it's going to be hot pink?" I checked.

He lifted a shoulder. "We won't know until it's finished changing."

I picked up a chunk of it and studied the color closely. The pink was definitely getting richer.

"Your eyes are changing too," he added. "They're looking purple."

"*Purple*?" My eyebrows shot upward. "How purple?"

He leaned closer, studying them. After a moment, he leaned back. "Very purple. And they've started to glow a little"

Hot damn.

"Will there be light in our den when we get back to your pack? So I can see?"

"The huvim will be attracted to your magic, so yes. Though I imagine your sight in the dark will be much better by that point, as well."

Well, I definitely wouldn't complain about being able to see better. Especially if they didn't have lightbulbs in Evare.

"I believe I mentioned before that you will have your own den, if you prefer it," Amarok added, studying me closely as he finally took a bite of his own fruit.

Relief relaxed my shoulders.

He had mentioned it, but I was worried I had heard him wrong or that he'd change his mind or something. "I would definitely prefer it."

He nodded. "You need time to grow acquainted with life in Evare, and I understand that, Rory. I will not push you for anything you are not ready to give."

My throat swelled.

Green flag.

That had to be a green flag.

It didn't wipe away the red flag of the insane possessiveness he had mentioned, but still.

I hadn't been planning on mentioning the friendship thing until we got back to his pack, but honestly, I felt like he deserved to know. He wasn't trying to push me, and he was making it clear that I would determine the pace of our relationship, if we had one.

"You mentioned before that some mates are just friends," I said.

"Yes. It's not common, but it happens."

I nodded. "What would you say, if I said I only wanted us to be friends?"

"I would hope for more, over time, but would accept friendship without question if that was all you were willing to give." After a moment of hesitation, he admitted, "If my packmates and I were willing to accept a life of friendship, we could've mated with each other centuries ago to defeat immis. Friendship isn't what any of us are after, in the long run. But we are old enough to wait a few more centuries for our females to be ready, if we must."

My throat swelled.

He wanted more than a friend.

It would be awful for me to drag him along on a fraction of hope that I might eventually have more feelings for him.

I wanted love, but I didn't know how long it would be until I was ready. It would be cruel for me to ask him to wait for me when I wasn't entirely sure how long I would need. So... I would have to make it clear to him that I wasn't looking for a mate.

"I don't know if I'll ever be ready for anything more than friendship, Amarok. I think you should pursue other women, after our bond is broken. Or before, if you can."

A low growl rumbled his chest, but I'd heard him growl enough times that it didn't scare me. "A male shifter would never consider another female while he was bound to one in any capacity, Rory."

Shit.

I opened my mouth to apologize, but before I got the words out, he said, "Even after our bond breaks, I will be yours. Fate has declared it so, and I trust in fate. I will give you as much time as you need to heal, then I will pursue you as a human male would."

My face flushed. "That doesn't mean I'm going to fall in bed with you."

"Of course not. It means I won't give up until your heart belongs to me, and no one else."

There was that damn possessiveness again. "What if I wanted a different man?"

The darkness in his eyes grew deeper and thicker. "Then he would die, swiftly."

Whatever I'd been about to say stuck in my throat like a big lump.

"Eat, Rory. You need your strength," he warned me.

I no longer had an appetite, but I forced myself to take another bite... if just to keep myself from fighting with him.

There wasn't a green flag in Evare that could overpower the massive red of his possessiveness.

THE WOODS WEREN'T AS cold as the Peaks at night, so I managed to sleep on my own with minimal tossing and turning. My skin was coated in a layer of the strange red dirt that covered the ground in the Woods, making me severely uncomfortable, but I'd survive.

I always had before, after all.

When morning came around, my mood was a bit darker. The running we did brightened it, though, and I managed not to let my mind linger *too* long on our conversation the night before. Or the fact that it sounded like I was trapped in a bond with Amarok whether I wanted to be or not.

I gave short answers when he started a conversation that night, and he got the message that I didn't want to talk, so we went to sleep fairly soon after stopping.

. . .

THE NEXT NIGHT, we finally reached his pack.

The trees changed around us as we approached their land, going from red and black to the typical shades of trees on Earth. The trunks were brown, the leaves were green, and flowers blossomed everywhere.

Some part of me relaxed at the familiarity, even though I wouldn't have gone back to Earth by choice for anything.

A few wolves joined us as we ran through the brown and green trees, all of them in shades of black, white, and gray.

When he spoke into my mind to let me know we'd reached the center of the pack's land, we turned a wide corner. In front of us, I found a group of three women, surrounded by a handful of men.

My eyes widened as I took them in.

Amarok slowed to a stop, and I couldn't help as my grip tightened in his fur. Not because of the women, but because of the men.

They all looked like Amarok.

Massively tall, covered in an outrageous number of tattoos, and insanely muscled.

Suddenly, the wolf beneath me seemed much, much safer than the ones in front of me.

Amarok shifted forms and smoothly tucked me against his side. As much as I didn't want to cling to him for safety, I found myself pressing against him. His grip on me was secure, and it calmed me a little.

The hot pink of my hair was sandwiched between us, bright and vibrant.

One of the other guys tossed Amarok a pair of shorts, and he pulled them on with one hand, holding me with the other arm.

The woman at the front of the group spoke, and my gaze jerked to her. Her hair was bright red, her skin was somewhere between pale and tan, and she looked tiny next to the man whose arm was wrapped lazily around her hip. Her side rested against his with a confidence I immediately envied.

She was comfortable with him, in a way I didn't think I'd ever been comfortable with anyone. Definitely not with any man.

She grinned broadly at me. "Welcome to the Woods Pack. I'm Ezra, and this is my mate, Ivaylo. We're the alphas here."

"Hi," I managed.

I silently pleaded with Amarok to do the introducing and whatever else there was to do, for me.

He couldn't hear, of course.

After a moment of silence, he spoke anyway. "This is Rory, my fated mate. She would feel safest in a den of her own, surrounded by those belonging to the other unmated females."

Relief had me sagging slightly, and leaning further into Amarok's side.

"Of course." Ezra glanced at the other two women, and my gaze flitted over them quickly. One had neon-yellow hair and olive skin, and the other's hair was a pastel green color, her skin dark.

All three of them strode toward me, and the tightness in my stomach eased slightly.

They were going to have my back, I hoped.

Ezra's mate, Ivaylo, stayed beside the other men, and didn't look at all annoyed that his woman had just walked away from him without an explanation. I wasn't sure what to think about that, but it did seem like a good thing.

If I'd walked away from Allen like that, there would've been hell to pay.

"This way." The green-haired girl tilted her head to the left, clearly telling me that was where we needed to go. When she started walking in that direction, Amarok's grip on me loosened slightly.

I grabbed his arm and held on tight as I took the first few steps after them.

He didn't say a word, walking at my side silently as I followed the women.

"We all know it's intense to get here at first," the yellow-haired woman offered. "The guys are kind of terrifying before you understand how their society works. Then, they're just big, sexy teddy bears."

I glanced over at Amarok, found his gaze lingering on me, and quickly looked back to the women in front of me.

The big, sexy teddy bear thing honestly fit what I had seen of him, for the most part.

"Being fated will make the transition easier, too," the green-haired woman added. "I'm Riley, by the way."

"I'm Jill," the yellow-haired one said. "Is Rory short for something?"

"Aurora," I admitted. "My mom was obsessed with fairy-tales, before the drugs took over."

"I love that." Riley flashed me a smile. "Who doesn't want to be named after a princess?"

I couldn't help the small curve of my lips. "It was cool, when I was five."

All three women laughed, and my smile grew slightly.

I hadn't had friends in so damn long.

RORY

"BEING FATED with Rok is honestly going to make this whole thing much easier for you," Jill said. I assumed Rok was Amarok's nickname, and was a little irked he hadn't told me that.

Was he close with her in some way?

"Ezra has told us all how simple everything was for her and Ivaylo. It kind of makes us want to grab her by the hair and shake her," she explained.

A laugh escaped me, and Ezra gave Jill a playful push. The contact was so light, Jill didn't even stumble as we continued walking through the trees, but it made her grin.

"Not *simple*," Ezra corrected. "Just *different*."

"Different how?" I asked, my voice curious.

"There are forty-eight single werewolves right now," Ezra said, gesturing to the forest. Amarok growled, and she corrected herself. "Forty-*seven* single werewolves."

My gaze followed her hand, and when I did a double-take, I realized there were at least a dozen wolves in the trees around us, just following us through the forest.

"There are only four potential mates, including you. There are six of us women here, total, but I'm mated, and Amy finally bit Ax last week, sealing their bond. Because you're fated to Rok, and the eclipse is coming up, the other guys will realistically leave you alone for the next three and a half months or so."

Riley and Jill nodded their agreement as we kept walking.

"What do you mean, leave me alone?" I asked.

"Ezra opened her big mouth and told the guys that humans choose their mate after dating to get to know them, so we all have suitors. Many, many suitors." Jill tossed a hand toward the forest again.

"She's exaggerating," Riley said. "The guys are all really sweet, they're just all looking for someone to settle down with."

"Pause a second," Ezra said, stopping. Everyone else followed her lead. "Will you be more comfortable living in a small, cozy space, a wide open one, or something between the two?"

I glanced at Amarok, and he met my gaze but didn't answer the question for me.

He wanted *me* to choose.

The part of me that had yearned for freedom for so long wanted me to say *wide open*, but it didn't feel honest. Smaller spaces usually made me feel the safest, truthfully.

"Cozy," I admitted.

"Perfect." Ezra resumed walking, and the rest of us did too.

"The guys are all looking for someone to spend eternity with," Riley said, resuming her explanation. "Most of us didn't come here looking for love, so they're trying to convince us. But there's a lot of competition for it, because of the guy to girl ratio."

"We're basically living in The Bachelor," Jill clarified. "There's always someone taking us out, trying to win our hearts. Fights break out over us if we're not clear enough about how we feel. We have to reject the guys we're not interested in, and let the ones we might be pursue us, or at least befriend us."

My face warmed.

Had Amarok been rejected by any of them?

I couldn't help but glance over at him.

"I was waiting for my fated female," he said into my mind, his gaze steady on mine. I remembered him saying he was patrolling in the Peaks when Serae transported me in, or something along those lines, so it did check out.

"About a dozen of the guys decided they aren't playing the Bachelor game," Riley said. "They're waiting for their fated mates. They've spread out through the entirety of the Broken Woods, set on finding the women wherever and whenever Serae appears with them. She's a bit unpredictable."

Jill snorted. "A *bit*."

"She's a hot mess," Ezra agreed. "But she did get us here, so that counts for something."

The other two women nodded, and they finally stopped in front of what looked like a... door. In the ground?

I frowned down at it.

"The guys are still working on clearing out some of the old dens and getting them ready for new women," Riley explained, gesturing to the door in the ground. "They usually conceal the entrances with trees or massive boulders, but they haven't had time yet. So, the entrances look like this. They're more secure than they look. This one's cozy and open, so, welcome home!"

Oh.

Okay.

I forced a smile, my fingers digging into Amarok's arm just a little harder. They were giving me my own place to live, so I needed to be grateful. Much, much more grateful than I was in that moment.

Ezra pried the thick wooden slab up off the dirt with Jill's help, and I peered down into a hole.

It wasn't even a glorified hole; it was a straight-up hole.

My stomach clenched.

"There's a ladder," Jill told me, probably seeing the worry written all over my face.

"Historically, wolves didn't let anyone but their mates in their dens," Ezra explained, flopping the door closed. "Scent is one of those things that can really affect the guys, so we try to keep with the tradition. We give every woman her own den, but we also have a larger den for the whole pack, where the guys tend to hang out. There's a smaller one for the women, too."

"Maybe let's go to the women's one?" I asked, still nervous. The last thing I wanted to do was climb into a hole all alone. What if there was a guy in there, waiting to attack me?

It wasn't likely, but... still.

"Sounds good," Ezra agreed. "Sorry, we're awkward at this. Still trying to figure out the best way to welcome new women."

"It's just an awkward transition, I think," I admitted as we resumed walking. I tried to remember where the flap for the den was, but all the trees looked so similar, I doubted I'd be able to really cement it in my mind.

"It is," all three of the women agreed.

My shoulders relaxed slightly when we walked up to what basically resembled a huge log cabin. It was big enough that I would've called it a mansion more than a cabin, but cabins came in all shapes and sizes, right?

At least it was a house-like structure.

That alone made it feel more like home.

Jill and Riley strode into the cabin like they'd done it a thousand times, and Ezra waited outside, near the door.

"You'll have to let go," Amarok murmured into my mind, as we stopped.

Oh.

Right.

Fear swelled in my throat, and I forced my fingers to unlock from his arm, slowly prying them off his skin. My eyes widened when I saw how red his skin was beneath my grip, and noticed four small, crescent-shaped cuts.

My fingernails had made the poor man bleed.

I couldn't stop myself from tensing, or hold back the panic that swelled in my chest.

"Sorry," I said quickly, my gaze flicking to his.

Where I expected to find fury, I found only the intense warmth of his gorgeous, dark eyes. *"Never apologize for holding on to me when you are afraid. My blood doesn't bother me, Aurora."*

Ohh.

I kind of liked the way he used my whole name. No one had called me that since I was a kid.

"There's only one door that functions as an exit and an entrance. I'll be waiting out here, in case you need me." His fingers brushed my arm gently, and then he took a step back.

I didn't like the space. Not even a little bit.

"You don't need to wait here," I whispered. "I'm fine."

"I never said you weren't." His lips lifted in a slow, small smile.

"You could go back to your den and shower. I'm sure you feel as disgusting as I do, right now."

"I won't be going home again until you're going with me." He shifted forms, and my worry faded slightly.

"I told you, I'm not taking a mate for anything other than friendship."

"I haven't forgotten." He brushed his furry side against my smooth one.

My face flushed, but I turned around and slipped into the women's den. Ezra followed me, closing the door unceremoniously behind us.

I found myself standing in a massive, open space with a living room and a kitchen that rolled into each other.

My stomach clenched, and I felt more sure than ever about wanting a cozy den.

Jill and Riley were already in the kitchen, cooking. It had to be late for dinner, but no one was complaining.

"I thought women don't cook here," I said, as I walked with Ezra to a row of stools in the kitchen.

"Not for their mates," Ezra agreed. "In the Peaks, they don't cook at all. We've been forcing the men to wrap their minds around the fact that we can cook for them too sometimes."

Huh.

"What do the women in the Peaks do, then?" I asked. "Not that cooking is all they'd do otherwise. I just mean—"

"We've got you." Ezra flashed me a grin. "The dynamic is weird, we know. The whole idea in the Peaks is that the men take care of the women, and the women bring joy to the men in exchange. So the guys make dinner, and the ladies make desserts. The guys create functional clothes, the women make fun ones. The guys build houses, the women decorate them, and make art for them."

I blinked.

"The guys in the Woods have been alone so long that some of those traditions have already faded. You've seen the tattoos on them; a handful of the guys are artists. We're slowly making the tasks more equal around here, but it will never be Earth."

"Thank the damn veil for that," Jill called out.

My lips curved upward. "What is the veil? I've heard Amarok mention it before. He tried to explain a lot of things, but I think he didn't realize some of them didn't make sense to me."

Ezra nodded. "Rok's one of the good ones. He's Ivaylo's beta, along with Valko. The three of them basically held the pack together over the last fifty years. Their numbers dwindled pretty fast after the last alpha lost his fight to immis."

I blinked.

Ezra clearly understood a hell of a lot more of the pack's history than I did. I knew basically nothing.

"The veil separates this world and this life from the ones before and after. I wouldn't be so inclined to believe in it, but Serae said she had to cross it to find Earth, so... I'm a believer," Ezra said.

"Most of us are," Riley agreed. "But no one will be offended if you aren't, so don't worry about it."

I bit my lip, but nodded. I had no idea what I believed.

"Tell us about yourself, Rory," Ezra said, leaning over the countertop in front of us. Her gaze was interested. "And about your trip here. From the amount of dirt on your skin, I assume it was a long one."

My face warmed. "There's not a whole lot to tell. My parents were addicts, so I graduated early and went into nursing. I ignored the red flags, and ended up in an abusive relationship with a cop. Tried to leave a handful of times, but he had too much of a grip on me. No one ever believed me enough to get involved, and my family wasn't there to help. He was going to kill me, if I tried again. I'd basically given up when Serae appeared next to me on a bench and brought me here."

Riley and Jill continued cooking, but their eyes and Ezra's were on me enough that I kept talking, telling them how I'd waited in the Peaks and Amarok had found me.

They told me their stories afterward, and we shared a meal together. I learned that Ezra had lost the only people she loved after a long battle with cancer. Jill had grown up in a trailer park, abused in every way there was, but was stronger because of it, and Riley's ex had stolen everything from her and disappeared a few weeks before she was brought to Evare.

Talking to them, I realized something.

Something big, and important.

I wasn't the only one there who had suffered. All of us had been through our own struggles, and we had all survived.

Maybe even more important than that, though, was the fact that we'd made it to Evare. All three of them agreed vocally that life in the pack was simple, and peaceful. That they were cared for and protected, no matter what.

I wasn't sure exactly what to do with that information, but it made me feel much, much more comfortable with where I was.

AFTER WE FINISHED EATING, I felt more confident in my ability to handle moving into my own den, so I headed out to find the door again. All three of the other women went with me, looking for their men. Jill and Riley admitted they were both exclusively dating their own wolf shifters, and Ezra winked at me and said they'd be mated in no time.

My face heated. I felt bad that I had no intentions of sealing the bond with Amarok, but I had been clear about that since the beginning, so it was what it was.

Amarok would have to find a way to survive without me, because he wasn't willing to settle on friendship, and I wasn't willing to consider anything else.

seven

AMAROK

I TOSSED a shovel full of dirt onto the pile behind us, and my head jerked to the side as I heard the door to the women's den open.

Eril and Tehr hauled themselves out of the pit, abandoning their shovels as they strode toward the den. I dropped mine and walked with them, shifting forms as I went. Their females were used to nudity, but mine was not.

"See you later," Ezra called to the other women, heading off toward the shop Ivaylo was working on with a few of our other males.

"Have fun." Jill stuck her fist out toward Riley, who bumped her own fist against it. When she moved her fist toward Rory, my female only hesitated a moment before doing the same.

A tentative smile curled her lips, making me really damn glad she had gone with them.

As much as I despised being away from her, she needed to know she belonged in the pack just as much as anyone else.

I reached her as my brothers pulled their females into their arms, and brushed my side against hers in greeting, knowing anything more would make her uncomfortable.

It would take time to make her see that I would never hurt her like Allen had, but she would realize soon enough. Even if it took years, I wasn't moving a damn inch.

She was mine.

Fate had declared it, and I had decided it.

Now, there was no going back for me.

"Can you show me where my den is?" she asked me, her voice soft and uncertain as she lightly brushed her hand over the top of my head. "I think I'll sleep there tonight."

"Of course."

Her fingers buried deeper into my fur, and she held on loosely, walking beside me as I started toward her den.

"The females were kind to you?" I asked, unable to stop myself. Though I trusted them for the most part, my mate needed to be welcomed with warm, open arms so she didn't feel the way she had on Earth. She needed to understand that she was loved and wanted.

"They were great," she admitted.

Satisfaction eased my mind. *"I'm glad."*

"Me too." Her grip loosened, and her fingers brushed lightly through my fur. "You need a shower."

I made a noise of agreement.

"Jill and Riley said I should be careful not to go into your den, or let you into mine. They said it had something to do with scent. Ezra disagreed, and thought it would be fine if I went into your den, but said I shouldn't let you into mine unless I was ready to accept you as my mate."

I made a noncommittal noise. *"Having a female's scent in a male's den will drive him to think about her more and want her more. The unmated females warned you against it, because they're still considering multiple males. They haven't committed to my brothers, so they stay out of their dens to prevent them from growing too attached. Ezra sees no point in you staying out of my den, because she understands the importance of fate's decisions to us."*

"What does that mean?"

"In the past, a female allowing a male into her den would be her way of declaring her intentions toward him. No other male would go near her. If she decided to bring another man in, the scent of the first would drive the second to violence."

Her eyebrows shot upward. "Damn."

"A male wolf takes fate's decision very, very seriously. Only three men in our history have ever not sealed a bond with the women fate led them to, and it was because the females refused them based on their past actions."

"So Ezra thinks you're already set on me enough that there's no point in staying out of your den, because the damage is already done on that front."

"Correct."

Her lips pressed together, and I saw frustration on her face. Uncertain what I could say to ease it, I remained quiet until we reached her den. I would need to surround it with boulders or place a large tree over it, to secure it, but I would have to wait until she was willing to do so with me, because I wasn't comfortable enough to leave her alone for that long.

I grabbed the slab of wood in my jaws and hauled it upward, opening it for her. *"The pack eats breakfast early, but sleep as long as you want. I can cook for you whenever you're ready."*

Red stained her cheeks, contrasting beautifully with the vibrant pink of her hair. "Thanks."

"Of course. Climb down carefully; if you are hurt, I will come in to check on you, consequences be damned."

The red on her cheeks deepened. "Alright."

With that, she eased herself onto the ladder and slowly began her descent. A moment later, I heard her feet hit the floor, and she called out quietly, "You can close it. Thank you."

"If you need anything, let me know. I'll be right outside all night."

"You should go home and shower," she protested.

I closed the slab in response, saying nothing to her suggestion.

There wasn't a thing in our world that could drag me from her side. After centuries of waiting, I had finally found my female. I was nowhere near foolish enough to walk away from her after so damn long without her.

Over time, I would prove myself to her, and she would accept that fate was correct. I would love her in ways no other male ever could—and I would protect her just as much.

RORY

MY FACE WAS STILL BURNING when I turned around at the bottom of the ladder, and peered around the den I'd been given. Or assigned, maybe. My vision was already much, much better than it had ever been in the dark before. I could make out the colors and shapes almost as easily as I could during the day.

As I took everything in, my shoulders relaxed.

It was perfect.

The space reminded me of a comfy studio apartment, with a simple, nice kitchen, a large bed up against a wall, and a bathroom and closet on another wall. There was enough space that it didn't feel squished, but not so much that I wouldn't feel at ease.

I pulled the lever Amarok told me would lock the den, and watched a thick stone plate slide into place over the opening above my head.

It made me feel much more secure, and relaxed me further.

When I checked the kitchen, I found it stocked with equipment, but no food. I stepped into the closet afterward, and my lips curved upward when I found a similar variety of clothing to what we'd found with the other pack. There was a row of bodysuits and massive tees in multiple sizes.

There was a note stuck to the wall behind the clothes, too, with some kind of sap securing it. It was clearly written in a woman's handwriting, and said:

> Welcome to the pack!
> The women's den is stocked ridiculously well.
> Bring whatever you don't like or want back to the den and swap it out!
>   <3 Ezra

I bit my lip to stop myself from smiling. When I realized there was no reason to do so, I released my lip from between my teeth.

My smile widened as I slipped out of the closet and into the bathroom. After I was clean, I'd try everything on so I could decide what I wanted and didn't want. The next day, I would go to the den and swap it out for more of what I liked.

In the bathroom, I found everything I needed, and it was all labeled.

There was another note attached to something that mostly resembled a razor on the countertop. The note explained that shifter men and women didn't give a damn about natural body hair, but it was there in case I wanted it.

My smile widened, and I left it there.

Allen had been disgusted by body hair. It was a constant battle to keep myself smooth; a battle I no longer had to fight.

I'd embrace the hell out of my hairy legs and arms.

I glanced back at the razor as I stepped in the shower, and remembered the prickliness in my armpits...

Maybe I would shave *them*.

But nothing else.

I found myself humming a tune to a song whose name I couldn't even remember as I scrubbed myself clean. The clothes I'd worn for our journey were so dirty, I would take joy in throwing them away. None of the men or women in the pack seemed to wear shoes, so my high-tops could go too.

It was a fresh start, in a way I'd never thought I would get one, but had needed for so damn long.

As my fingers scrubbed my scalp and worked through my hair, I couldn't help the annoyance that bubbled up as my mind went back to my Earth life.

Allen had told me I needed long hair to cover my many imperfections. It distracted from my unattractive qualities, he'd said.

Screw Allen.

No…

Fuck Allen.

He could go straight to hell for all I cared.

I didn't need long hair, or anything else to hide my body. I was good enough, flaws and all.

That determination and certainty followed me all the way to bed, and stuck with me while I slept alone, in the bed and home that were now mine, and no one else's.

WHEN THE NEXT morning came around, I went through the clothes in the closet, then unlocked the den and hauled the ones that didn't work for me back up the ladder.

The other women had made up their own sizes for clothing, which made me grin. Rather than having small, medium, large, and so forth, they labeled them with colors. Turquoise, magenta, lavender, hot pink, bright red, and a few others. I was a hot pink, which only made my grin wider.

As he'd promised he would be, Amarok was waiting at the top. He had opened the wooden cover as soon as I unlocked the den, so I had no problem getting through.

He shifted to his man form and took the stack of clothing from my hand before I cleared the ledge, then closed the wood slab with his foot for me.

I didn't let my eyes move to his erection, or catch on the glow around him whose reason I still didn't know. He was gorgeous, but I couldn't let myself care about that.

Being pretty didn't erase the possessiveness, or the potential damage that possessiveness could do to me.

Eventually, I would need to ask him about the glowing.

Or... maybe I could ask the other women.

Yes, that was a much better idea.

"You're gorgeous in my people's clothing, Aurora," Amarok told me, as we started walking toward the women's den. Some part of me knew exactly which direction I needed to walk in to find it, and I didn't question that.

"Thank you." My cheeks were a little warm, so I didn't let myself look over at him. If I let myself look at him for long, I would inevitably grow attracted to him, which I could not afford.

"Will you let me cook for you?" he asked me, as we walked.

"No thanks. I'm going to eat at the women's den today. You could shower while I'm there, too. If it makes it easier for you, I can promise not to leave until you're back."

His chest rumbled unhappily. "No. I'm not comfortable walking away from you."

Okay, then.

"Alright. I might be there a while."

"I don't mind the wait."

That was that, then.

Despite our uncomfortable conversation, excitement fluttered in my chest.

When I went back to my den that night, I was going to look and feel like an entirely different person. I'd say goodbye to Allen and his control over me for the final time.

There was a chance Amarok would lose his shit at me when I did, but if so, screw him too. I was done with possessive, controlling men. It was time to be me, and no one and nothing else.

When we reached the women's den, I plucked the pile of clothes from Amarok's grasp. "Thank you. I'll see you later, I guess."

He dipped his head, and didn't say a word or try to stop me as I slipped into the building.

A woman I didn't recognize with bright purple hair and dark skin was curled up on a couch with a book, and she flashed me a smile as the door closed behind me. "You're the new girl?"

"Yeah, I'm Rory." I mirrored her smile.

"Nice to meet you. I'm Kyla. I hear you're fated to Rok."

Geez, did he tell *everyone* to call him by his nickname except me?

Obviously, he didn't feel as attached to me as he said.

"Seems like it," I agreed. "I don't plan on sealing the bond, though. I'm not looking for love right now. Just friendship."

Kyla's smile widened. "Me too. The guys can't seem to accept that, so I spend most of my time holed up in here or at my den."

"I don't blame you," I admitted. "I'll probably do the same thing when I'm settled enough."

She nodded. "What are your plans for the day?"

"I've got to swap these clothes out for some that fit, and I need to learn how to cook with the ingredients here so I don't have to rely on the guys for that, too."

"Oh, Jill and Ezra had the guys help them make a cookbook. They put one in every den; I'll show you." She put her book down and led me into the kitchen. I set my pile of clothes down on a clean bit of countertop, and followed her over to one of the cabinets near the Evare version of a fridge.

When she pulled out a thick book, my eyebrows lifted. I accepted it and flipped through, finding drawings of different kinds of ingredients that said what everything was. Many recipes followed, and something within me settled as I looked through them.

"Thank you," I finally said, closing the book and putting it back.

"No problem. The transition is weird for all of us." Kyla leaned back against some of the cabinets, not seeming like she was in a hurry to go back to her book.

I felt more at ease with her, knowing she felt the same way I did about not wanting a mate. "Can I ask you something?"

"Of course."

"Do you know why Amarok glows?"

Her smile faded a little. "He didn't tell you?"

"He said he didn't think I wanted to know. I didn't—and don't," I admitted. "But it seems like it's probably important."

"Yeah, the glow is a part of something the guys call *the frenzy*. You should probably be glad it's not affecting you."

I frowned.

"Basically, the men have magic in their chest that ignites when nature or fate determines it's the right time. Amy was dating one of the shifters seriously for a month and a half before his magic ignited. When the magic ignites, it takes control of the guy completely, and starts something they call a mate run. The mate run is fueled by the frenzy magic, and it drives him to run to the woman fate has chosen for him. When he reaches her, he bites her. The bite starts the bond, as you know, but the frenzy magic doesn't fade until the bond has either been sealed by the woman biting him back, or broken by the eclipse."

I blinked.

"After the guy bites the girl, the frenzy becomes hers as well, and it wraps around her, making her glow too. How much it glows is determined by how attracted they are to each other. Since you're not glowing, it's safe for everyone to assume you're not attracted to Rok, or you at least don't want him physically."

I blinked again, a few more times.

Hot damn, that was a lot to take in.

"What happens if I never glow?" I asked her.

She lifted a shoulder. "I don't know. There's a decent chance some of the guys will start pursuing you as soon as the bond is broken, if you're clearly not interested in Rok."

Shit.

"Ezra told me I'd probably have three months after the eclipse before any of the other guys would try to hit on me."

Kyla's lips curved upward. "If the guys agreed to logic, probably."

But they weren't logical.

And they all wanted mates, except the dozen who were out in the Woods, waiting for more women to be brought from Earth.

"So if I never glow, they'll think Rok failed or isn't right for me."

"More like they'll see it as an opportunity to have a chance with you. And some of those bastards are very, very persistent."

I let out a long breath. "Guess I'm going to have to figure out how to make myself glow."

"Just be careful with it, if you do. Ezra says that when you glow, you get warm and horny."

Great.

That was just great.

I made a face, and Kyla laughed. "It's not so bad. At least we're not on Earth anymore."

"That is a very, very good point." I glanced around the kitchen. "Have you seen any scissors, by chance? I decided I'm going to cut my hair off."

Her eyebrows shot upward. "Damn, girl. New world, new hair?"

"Something like that." I flashed her a smile. "Want to help?"

Her lips stretched in a wicked grin. "Hell, yes."

RORY

THIRTY MINUTES LATER, I was sitting on a kitchen chair in the bathroom, my knees squished to my chest as Kyla chopped a bit next to my ear.

I stared at myself in the mirror, trying to wrap my mind around the new look.

The longest pieces of my hair fell to the middle of my neck, and it was shorter in the back. The cut definitely wasn't symmetrical, or even in any way, but it was there.

And hot damn, I looked different.

Stronger.

Bolder.

Free.

I looked free.

I lifted my trembling fingers to the length of it, and watched in the mirror as my fingers slipped through the soft, short ends.

"What the hell did you do?" Ezra's shocked voice made both of our heads jerk to the doorway of the bathroom.

"She wanted a haircut," Kyla said, at the same time I said,

"I needed a change."

Our eyes met for a moment, and we both burst out laughing.

It wasn't even that funny, but damn, we laughed until tears were streaking down our faces. Ezra looked at us like we were insane, until she finally snagged the large kitchen scissors from Kyla.

"You guys are insane. You know most of the men have been cutting each other's hair for centuries, right? Pretty much any of them could've done this for you, and then it wouldn't be so..." she trailed off.

"Messy?" Kyla suggested helpfully.

"Jagged?" I supplied.

"Uneven?" Kyla added.

"All of the above," she agreed.

"I like it," I said, turning back to the mirror and turning my head.

Yeah, it would be better without some of the protruding long chunks, and maybe with some layers so the ends didn't look so thick and chunky. But it was still so different, I couldn't help but love it.

I wasn't my old self anymore. It was time to be Rory 2.0. The fiercer, more real version of myself. The version no one else could ever control.

"Want me to ask Ivaylo to fix it?" Ezra checked. "Er, even it out?"

Ivaylo was her gigantic mate, with the light gray eyes and shaggy hair. Did I want his hands in my hair?

Hell no.

I nearly shuddered at the idea.

"I don't think that would be a good call, considering the possessive furball waiting for her outside." Kyla gestured toward the exit.

Right.

That damn possessiveness.

"Hmm. Good point." She studied me. "We could ask Rok."

"No, we couldn't," I said quickly.

Her eyes narrowed, but I didn't think her sudden suspicion was pointed at me. "He hasn't done anything to hurt you, right?"

"Oh, no. Definitely not. I feel a lot safer with him than any of the other guys," I said quickly. "I just don't want his hands in my hair. I'm not sure how my body will react. I try not to look too closely at him."

She gave me a knowing grin. "No wonder you're not glowing."

My face heated, the red looking more vibrant next to the pink of my hair.

Damn, that was terrible luck. Maybe I should've left it long.

My gaze moved over the short, choppy strands.

No, the length was perfect.

"I'm just going to leave it," I decided. "It's a lot better than it was. I feel ten pounds lighter, so thank you, Kyla."

"No problem." She gave me a quick hug, and I returned it.

"Worren brought you cake," Ezra told Kyla.

Her eyes lit up, and I wondered if she was really as against being pursued by the werewolves as she claimed.

"Gotta go!" She hurried out of the bathroom, and Ezra moved to the side to let her past.

I stood up, brushing the long strands off my arms and legs. She came back with the broom, and I swept the hair up quickly, unable to stop the grin that blossomed on my face as I said goodbye to the hair. It was just hair... but it felt like so much more.

It felt like freedom.

"I'm heading home to shower," I told her, after I finished cleaning up, then ducked into the room of spare clothes and grabbed a few more sets in my size.

"No worries. I brought you some groceries, so you should take them back home with you. The guys are still working on getting the grocery store up and running, but it takes forever for the produce to go bad here, so it's not really a priority," Ezra said, walking with me to the door. I found a few reusable bags waiting beside it, all of them loaded with food items.

"Thank you." I tucked my clothes in the top of the bag and then slipped out of the building.

Of course, Amarok was waiting outside for me. He shifted forms smoothly and took the bags for me, his gaze lingering on my face.

Probably on my haircut, actually.

"You're stunning with short hair," he said into my mind.

Shock made my eyes well with tears. I hadn't cut it to be attractive, but after hearing so many insults about how bad I'd look if I did, I hadn't expected anyone to like it. "Thank you."

"Don't thank me for being attracted to you."

My lips curved upward, but my mind went back to what Kyla had said about the glow.

And how I didn't glow.

It probably offended him that I wasn't glowing, yet he hadn't said a word about it. He hadn't brought it up, asked me about it, or done anything to try to make me glow.

Dammit, the man *respected* me. He respected that I had different feelings than him, and he wasn't trying to make me feel any certain way, even though we both knew it was what he wanted.

As difficult as it was to admit, from what I'd seen of Amarok, he was a good man.

And as much as I hated to say so, I was still basically punishing him for it.

He didn't ask me to stay outside, or request an invitation in when I reached my den. Instead, he simply lifted the sheet of wood and told me to be careful climbing down.

I put the extra clothes I'd grabbed away in the closet, then stepped into the bathroom.

My appearance caught me off guard once again when I saw it.

My hair was so different, and yeah, the hanging long pieces were worse than I'd realized in the bathroom at the women's den.

But it wasn't just my hair that was different; *I* was different too.

It was hard to wrap my mind around the reality of my situation, but in truth, everything had changed.

And in this new version of my world, love wasn't as simple as falling for someone and deciding to make a life with them. Fate was involved, and magic was too.

I may not have thought the same way the shifters did, but they were still intelligent beings with thoughts and emotions. The women I'd spoken with had more than proven that, and from what I gathered, all of them had wolf forms too.

If I continued refusing to really look at Amarok or consider him as a mate, I was going to create issues. Not just for myself, but for the whole pack, from what I'd gathered. The other men would try to pursue me, and he would feel a need to defend his claim on me.

So... I couldn't keep him at an arm's length, the way I had been doing. I needed to adjust my expectations and change the way I was living, to fit this new world I'd walked into.

And the only way I could do that was by having a conversation with him. A real, honest one.

One where I listened to what he was saying, and considered us connected in some way, like he did.

I let out a long breath.

I still needed a shower, but if I was going to have a serious conversation with him, it would be easier to do so while he was occupied. Then, I wouldn't get quite as overwhelmed. Why not ask him to be occupied fixing the random pieces of hair that had refused to work with us?

It felt like a massive decision, but it was settled.

So, I padded back to the ladder and pulled the lever to open the lock. "Are you good at trimming hair?" I called out. Both of us knew damn well that he was the only one up there, waiting for me, so I was obviously speaking to him.

"Passable," he said. *"Better with curly hair than straight. What are you hoping for?"*

My mind went back to his gorgeous, dark curls.

Damn, I was good at ignoring him and how attractive he was.

"I just want the long pieces cut to match the rest. It doesn't need to be perfect. Think you can handle that?"

"Of course. We can do it in the pack's den."

"Actually, I'd rather do it in your den, if you're comfortable with having me there."

I heard his satisfied rumble from where I stood, and my lips curved upward.

"I would like that tremendously."

"Perfect. I'm coming up now."

I climbed up, taking his outstretched hand for assistance as I cleared the top of the ladder. His eyes were smoldering as they met mine.

I gave him a small smile before he released my hand, and we started walking in a direction I hadn't been before.

"My den is near the center of the pack's land," he explained, speaking aloud to me for the first time in what felt like ages. "I'm one of Ivaylo's betas, and we were responsible for keeping an eye on the pack to watch for anyone who was losing their fight with immis."

"The betas help the alpha run the pack?" I checked, pretty sure that was what the other ladies had told me.

"Yes. Our role is minimal now that immis is barely a factor."

I nodded. "How did you keep people from losing their mind to immis?"

"We would drag them out of their dens and force them to do something with the rest of us, mainly. Keeping everyone sane was more about keeping everyone busy than anything else. When it got really bad, tradition was to get a new tattoo to distract yourself from the struggle."

Shit.

My heart hurt for them, if that was truly why they had so many tattoos.

"Why did you cut your hair?" he asked me, curiosity creeping into his voice.

My face warmed. "It felt like the final step toward freedom."

His forehead wrinkled just slightly, but he didn't push me for more information.

"I wanted to chop it for years. Allen said I would look hideous without my long hair, so I left it. Now, I'm here and away from him. Cutting it seemed like the best way to show myself that I'm finally physically free too."

"It takes a truly shallow male to consider a woman unattractive for her hair's length," Amarok said. "The more I learn about this bastard, the more certain I am that he would've been killed centuries ago if he were a shifter."

A soft laugh escaped me. "If shifters kill men who mistreat their women, yeah, he wouldn't have made it long. It feels good to be able to talk about it freely, though. I haven't had someone to talk to about him controlling me in a long, long time."

"You can always talk to me." The back of Amarok's hand brushed mine, and I got the impression he wanted to hold it. I wasn't quite ready for that, but I didn't move away from him.

"Thank you."

We walked in silence for another minute before I noticed a pair of large boulders nestled together. We'd passed a few others on our way, and I hadn't paid them any mind. However, we walked right on up to these ones.

"The boulders shield the den," Amarok explained. "The ladder is against the wall. Would you feel more comfortable going in before or after me?

I didn't particularly care, but I thought it was sweet that he asked, so I answered as honestly as possible. "After, I think."

He ducked into the space between the boulders, and dropped into the hole.

The sudden drop scared the hell out of me, and I scrambled to the edge, peering down to see if he was okay. "Amarok? What happened? Did you fall?"

"Male shifters don't need the ladders," he called back. "Sorry, I wasn't trying to scare you."

Geez, the bastard nearly gave me a heart attack.

"No worries." I eased my legs over the edge and started climbing down. He could probably see up my shirt, but the bodysuit covered enough of me that I wasn't too concerned by the possibility.

His hands landed lightly on my hips as I neared the bottom rung, and a soft squeak escaped me as he lifted me off the ladder and set me on my feet. It took me a moment to regain my balance, but when I turned, my eyes met his and lingered.

"You are stunningly beautiful," he murmured.

"Thank you." I brushed hair out of my eyes, and forced myself to look at him.

To really, really look at him.

At the chiseled jawline his face boasted, and the stubble growing on his chin.

At the neutral expression he wore, but the intensity in his gaze.

At the defined muscles on his arms, bare chest, and abdomen.

My body warmed, and slowly, a soft glow swelled around me.

His eyes widened fractionally, and the intensity in them grew hotter and deeper. His own glow brightened, seeming to pulse as it grew.

My face flushed, because now, I knew what the pulsing meant.

He was attracted to me.

He *wanted* me.

And... I wanted him too.

I just wasn't ready to act on it yet.

"Ready for that haircut?" he asked me, breaking the tense silence.

Thick relief rushed through me. "So ready."

His warm chuckle made me smile, just a little.

RORY

I FOLLOWED Amarok to the bathroom, silently checking out his den as we went. It was almost the exact same size as mine, but everything looked different.

The floors were shiny, made out of a light gray stone that must've been polished, and reminded me of fancy tile flooring back on Earth. The walls matched the floor, but the color was light enough that it made the space feel calmer and cozier rather than smaller.

His kitchen was the same size as my own, but everything was pristine, and like the floors, looked fancier. His bed was larger than mine, with thicker, fluffier blankets. His closet looked bigger too, though it was over half empty, from what I saw.

And when we walked into his bathroom, I nearly drooled at the sight of a monstrous bathtub that had been built into the ground. The thing almost looked like a small pool; it was at least the size of most hot tubs back on Earth, if not larger.

"Do you want me to sit or stand?" I asked him, as he opened a large, very-organized drawer and pulled out a pair of what were clearly hair scissors. I hadn't seen any chairs anywhere, or a kitchen table.

"Sit." He lifted me up onto the countertop, surprising me so much that a laugh escaped me.

"I forgot how much taller than me you are," I teased him lightly, as he pulled a wide comb through my hair. The short strands popped right through, but that didn't seem to bother him.

Then again, when I really thought about it, did anything seem to bother him? Even when I said no, he simply agreed with me.

"You just want me to even it out?" he asked, checking the rest of my hair.

"Yeah, trim the long pieces so nothing sticks out weirdly if you can. My hair is really straight, so anything that doesn't match will probably be really noticeable as soon as I wash it."

He nodded, then began.

We were both quiet, but it wasn't a tense or awkward silence. I didn't realize how comfortable I felt with him until I was relaxing while he had scissors so close to my face, truthfully.

More hair fell around me as he worked than I expected, but then again, I couldn't see the back. Maybe it was even worse than the front and sides.

Faster than I expected, he was checking the lengths of the pieces in the front with his fingers. My face warmed at his focus, but it didn't make me feel self-conscious. Honestly, it made me feel... cared for.

When he was satisfied that the sides matched, his thick fingers tousled the back of my hair. "It's even now, but it'll be better if I layer it a little."

"Okay, but not too much."

He made a noise of agreement, and I watched him work as he combed the strands out and up, cutting what almost looked like notches and taking weight out.

When he tousled the strands again, the difference was shocking. "It's gorgeous, Amarok."

"The hair isn't what's gorgeous here." His fingers toyed with the strands. I got the impression they did so because that was the only part of me I'd really given him permission to touch.

"Thank you," I said, blushing a little.

"For the compliment, or the haircut?"

"Both."

His lips curved downward slightly. "Humans thank their mates far more than they should."

"How can you thank someone too much?"

"A male is expected to care for his mate. Being thanked for doing so implies to him that he's doing something he's not expected to. It would be an insult, if she was a female shifter."

"I don't expect anyone to take care of me," I admitted. "At this point, it's a good day if no one insults me. I thank you because I feel grateful that you've treated me so well, when it's not at all what I expect or am used to."

"You deserve far more than I can give, Aurora." His hands landed lightly on my shoulders. "It nearly drives me to madness, knowing I can't kill the man who hurt you."

My face warmed further. "Murder isn't really accepted on Earth."

"What do you do with bastards like Allen, then?"

"If they're caught and there's enough evidence, they go to jail."

He scoffed. "Prison is a pointless sentiment among shifters. Why would you put time and effort into caring for someone who has proven themselves undeserving?"

"People change, sometimes," I said, but it felt like a lie.

"Some types of people, with some types of issues. Not someone who would hurt a female. That kind of man shouldn't be allowed to continue breathing."

Honestly, I couldn't say I disagreed with the sentiment. I had imagined myself killing Allen more times than I cared to admit, even though I'd never managed to bring myself to hurt him.

"If we were on Earth, I would thank you for freeing me from him, even if murder was the way you accomplished it."

"Since we aren't, tell me a way I can free you from him further," Amarok countered, finally setting his scissors back down.

I considered it.

His hands lifted back to my hair, though he hesitated for a moment, giving me a chance to tell him not to touch me. I liked the way his hands felt in it though, so I didn't say anything.

"Being my friend would help," I finally said. "Allen was really good at convincing me to distance myself from my friends until I didn't have anyone else. It would be nice to have a friend again. Someone I can trust. I already trust you for some reason, minus the possessive bit."

He tilted his head slightly, his lips curving downward like he didn't understand.

I could've kept quiet, but honestly, I *did* want to talk to him about it.

"Allen was possessive too," I explained. "About everything. He thought I was interested in another guy if I apologized for bumping into him at the grocery store. He didn't want me spending time with my friends, because he thought I loved them more than I loved him. Any time I brought up someone else, he assumed I was lusting after them. I couldn't talk to him about anything, or have friendships outside our relationship. I couldn't even *look* at anyone he might consider I could be attracted to when I was with him."

Amarok's hands resumed playing with my hair, and shit, it felt so good that the glow around me was getting a little brighter.

I didn't have the heart or willpower to ask him to stop.

"That sounds more like insecurity than possessiveness."

His words struck me, hard.

I guess it did.

"A mixture of both, then."

Amarok nodded. "Shifters are possessive, but not like that. If another male touched you, I would be driven to challenge him to a fight, not get angry with you. My possessiveness would drive me to not want other men to see you bare, and to satisfy you so thoroughly that I become your favorite. If I were the only man watching you unravel on my fingers, mouth, and cock, why would I feel insecure about you talking to your packmates and friends?"

My face flushed. "I have a hard time orgasming. I don't think I would want to have sex very often, even in the right relationship."

"Most females have a difficult time climaxing with an unskilled male. It would be different, with me."

I wasn't sure I believed him, but I couldn't exactly tell him he probably wasn't as good as he thought he was. What if he *was*? And geez, how many women had he been with to make him believe he was so damn wonderful at sex?

"We'll have to agree to disagree," I finally said, still flushed.

"Or you can simply agree to give me the chance to prove it to you," he countered.

My face flushed further.

Was he pushing me?

Was that a red flag?

It didn't feel like he was pushing me; it felt like he was *challenging* me.

And I kind of wanted to agree to his challenge.

"The eclipse will make us horny in a few weeks, right?" I asked.

"Extremely."

He had me curious with that one. "How extremely?"

"You will either spend the entire day with your hands between your thighs, or in my bed, letting me pleasure you."

"It's that strong?"

"It is."

I let out a long breath. "Alright, then. If you convince me that your idea of possessiveness is really how werewolves are, I'll let you try to prove yourself in bed during the eclipse."

"The eclipse isn't a time to prove anything. You'll climax much easier than usual, whether at your hands or mine."

I flushed redder.

His hands were in my hair, we were talking about sex, and it was making me all hot and bothered. There was no way it was healthy, but I was enjoying it anyway. Screw the red and green flags.

The words came out of my mouth before I had time to think them through. "Fine. Prove it now, then. If you can make me climax here, on this countertop, I'll have no choice but to believe you about your skills."

The glow around him flared, and he stepped closer until his body met my back. The thickness of his erection pressed lightly to my spine, and my own glow swelled alongside his.

His hands landed on my knees, his touch firm but gentle as he parted my thighs, opening me up to the mirror. I was still dressed in my t-shirt and bodysuit, but the man didn't seem to care.

Amarok's hands moved slowly up my legs, and my glow flared along with his as I shuddered.

Not in pain or horror, but because the way he touched me felt so good.

I hadn't enjoyed sex in so, so long. Hell, I couldn't even remember *enjoying* feeling a man's hands on my skin.

His thumbs moved slowly over the creases where my legs met my thighs. "Are you sure, Aurora?"

He was actually asking me what I wanted. Making sure I was okay with it before he touched me, even though I had already told him to do it.

Whatever existing trust I had in him grew rapidly.

"Yes, I'm sure."

My eyes were glued to the mirror as he slowly dragged his fingers between my thighs. I sucked in a breath when he touched my clit, and couldn't stop my hips from jerking a little.

His chest rumbled in satisfaction, and it made my head spin.

He found my clit, and focused on it. My breath hitched again at the touch, heat swelling within me. Amarok murmured, "How does that feel?"

He cared.

He actually *cared* about what I liked and wanted.

"Good," I whispered.

Amarok repeated the motion a bit harder, and my hips jerked again, more violently. "Better like that, or worse?"

"Still good, just different," I managed. "Equal."

He brushed me again, lighter. "And that?"

"Too soft."

I couldn't believe we were having the conversation, but it was happening, and shit, I liked it.

He worked my clit through the fabric a little, varying the pressure and watching my body closely in the mirror, to see how I responded. My breathing picked up, my body hot and needy, and I swear, there wasn't a damn thing I could do to stop myself from moving as he touched me.

Amarok was clearly in no hurry, the pleasure thick in his eyes as my bodysuit grew wetter by the moment. My desire grew thicker and thicker, until I finally got tired of waiting and said, "Take my clothes off."

After the command, my body went rigid.

Allen would never let me give him an order like that. I—

Amarok tugged my tee over my head.

My tension had faded slightly by the time it hit the floor, but when his hands gripped my breasts through the body-suit, it vanished entirely.

The way he squeezed me was perfect. Tight and needy, without causing me even the smallest amount of pain.

"You're still sure?" His gaze met mine in the mirror, and my attention left his hands and my body.

"Yes." There wasn't a shred of doubt left in my mind, at least when it came to what we were doing. He would take care of me—I trusted him to do that, as insane as it was.

His chest rumbled, and his hands lifted to the straps of my bodysuit.

Slowly, he pulled them down my arms, exposing my breasts and abdomen.

The glow around us both pulsed as he slid the fabric down further and further, until it joined my tee on the floor. My thighs started to close, but his hands caught them, and opened them wider.

"Do not hide from me, Aurora. I have waited centuries to see you like this." His growl was low, but not threatening.

And when his hands slid back up my thighs, the words died in my throat.

Slowly, he dragged a finger up the slickness of my center. I didn't think I'd ever been that wet in my life—and he definitely wasn't afraid of it.

"So damn ready for me," he murmured, teasing my entrance with his finger before sliding up to my clit.

I grabbed his arm for support as he teased it again, the way he had through my clothes. The sensation was insanely different without the fabric separating us—and so much better.

He worked me slowly, his gaze hot and intense as he watched me move and react to his touch. "How does that feel?"

"Incredible," I panted. "You know it's incredible."

"I wanted to hear you say it." His lips brushed my shoulder, where the healed claim mark shimmered silver. One of his hands slid up my abdomen. "Veil, your skin is soft." He caught one of my breasts in his hand and squeezed, making me gasp. "Especially here." He pressed harder on my clit. "And here." He moved his finger, and I cried out, bucking and digging my fingers into his arm at the intensity of it.

Easing up, he continued stroking me and teasing me. The pleasure was building so damn thickly, I felt like I was losing myself to it, in the very best way.

I wanted more, though.

I *needed* more, in a way I'd never needed anything.

"I want you," I moaned to him. "All of you."

"You'll have me for the rest of our lives, and long after we cross the veil," he growled back, dragging his teeth lightly over my shoulder as he worked me harder again, earning another cry. "But right now, this is about you, Aurora."

The words sent me over the ledge.

Desperate cries escaped me as I rocked and writhed against his hand while the pleasure crashed into me harder than it ever had before.

I came down from the high panting and dazed, with my hair in my face, my cheek against his bicep, and my chest rising and falling rapidly. Amarok still had my breast in one of his hands, and he was slowly working my clit even though I had already climaxed.

"Holy shit," I whispered. "You were right."

I didn't even care how many women he'd been with before me if *that* was the result. I'd even asked him to have full-on sex with me, and he'd refused, wanting nothing more than to touch me.

Amarok made a noise of agreement. "Have you ever climaxed twice in a row?"

eleven

RORY

MY EYES WIDENED. "NO."

His chest rumbled in satisfaction. "Three?"

"No..."

"Good."

His lips brushed the marking on my neck again. "I want you to watch me enter you with my finger, Aurora."

My entire body pulsed with need. "Okay."

Amarok gripped my thigh and opened my legs wider, exposing my slick folds to both of us more completely. My breathing was already picking up, and he was still touching my clit.

"You're stunning," he murmured. "Do you see how wet you are for me?"

"Yes," I nearly moaned.

Being so wet would've been a bad thing before, on Earth, with—

The thick tip of his finger brushed my opening, and my thoughts went silent as my gaze jerked to my core. His finger slowly stroked into me, thick and warm, and I cried out as it sank the rest of the way inside me.

"Veil, you are perfect," he growled into my ear.

My hips jerked with the compliment, and he moved his finger around, feeling me. My breaths grew more desperate, and my eyes remained on his hand as his thumb began working my clit again. He slid a second finger inside me, stretching me a little.

The pleasure was overwhelming, and I cried out as I shattered again, so much sooner than I had the first time.

My cheek pressed harder to his arm, my eyes closing as the pleasure faded.

His hands were still on my body, one still gripping my breast and anchoring me in place that way. "I want one more."

"Okay," I breathed—and then choked on that breath when he added a third finger to my channel and continued slowly working my clit.

It was torturously blissful.

The pleasure was absolutely insane.

But shit, I hoped it never ended.

Desperate noises I didn't know I was capable of making escaped me as he dragged me back to the edge. My hips jerked and my body rocked, the movements completely out of my control as my need swelled hotter.

When I finally shattered, I clenched around his fingers again and again, crying out in bliss at the pleasure.

"Oh damn," I panted, closing my eyes as I clutched his arm, still leaning against it with most of my weight. His fingers were still buried inside me, his thumb resting lightly on my clit. "You're right. You're very, very right."

His chest rumbled in satisfaction, and his lips brushed the base of my neck, where his mark lingered on my skin.

"I'm probably not as good in bed as whoever taught you how to do that," I said, heaving a sigh as I finally peeked my eyes open. They collided with his immediately.

"I learned in a group of males, in a class taught by an ancient mated shifter. So, neither am I. He had a long time to perfect his skills."

I blinked once, and then again. "You haven't..."

"No. Most shifters wait for their mates."

Shit.

Emotions warred within me, but I couldn't come up with a label for any of them. Instead, I slowly peeled a hand off his arm and reached backward.

"Don't, Aurora. This is about you," he said, his chest rumbling in warning.

I wrapped my hand around his erection through his shorts, and his eyes closed as his entire body shuddered. His fingers hooked inside me, and his thumb pressed harder on my clit.

The glow around both of us pulsed, and my curiosity thickened.

He had brought me pleasure on the bathroom counter, after I'd told him he wouldn't be able to...

Why couldn't I do the same for him?

"You don't have to do this." His voice strained.

"I know I don't." And if anything, that made me want to do it more.

He wouldn't hurt me if I didn't do what he wanted.

He wouldn't insult me.

Hell, he wouldn't do a damn thing even if I pulled my hand away like I was repulsed by him.

Amarok respected me, and had made me feel good, and I wanted to do the same for him.

"Can I touch you?" I asked him, realizing I hadn't asked him permission, like he had asked me.

"Anytime. Always. I belong to you; you never need to ask." He stumbled over the words enough that I felt... powerful.

I let go of his arm and turned, so my back was to the mirror. His hand moved with me, curling into my core a little harder. The pressure made me suck in a breath, but he wouldn't distract me from my goal.

Releasing his erection, I hooked my fingers in the waistband of his shorts and pushed them down. His cock sprung free, massive and dripping at the tip with his desire.

"I want you so badly," I whispered to him, wrapping my hand around his hardness.

He hissed, his thumb jerking against my clit and making my thighs clench around his hand. "I won't last long with my fingers buried inside you like this."

Heat flushed my entire body.

Getting me off had turned him on and brought him close to the edge. He *liked* making me feel good.

"Good. I want to watch you lose control," I said, stroking him.

His gaze was on my hand as I stroked him again, a little rougher. "You're going to end up with my release all over your soft skin if you keep that up."

That shouldn't have turned me on, but it did.

Having his fingers against my clit didn't hurt, either.

His breathing grew ragged as I continued stroking him. There was nothing between my hand and his cock except the slickness of his pleasure—but it was so damn slick, we didn't need anything else.

"Climax with me." His voice was low and commanding, his thumb flicking my clit in a slow rhythm that had my hips jerking and my breathing picking up.

He worked me faster with his thumb, and the pleasure built up before it finally detonated.

I lost control fast—so damn fast.

The pleasure hit hard—so damn hard.

My cries flooded the air, and his roars melded with them as he throbbed in my hand. The warm silk of his release coated my breasts, belly, and core while he lost control, and seeing him climax made my own last even longer than before.

Our chests rose and fell quickly, our gazes on each other's bodies. I could feel the heat of his eyes as they moved over my skin, taking in the sight of me coated in his release.

"You were right, it's different with you," I said, my voice only trembling slightly.

"I'm glad." He slowly slid his fingers out of my channel, and I had to bite my tongue to stop myself from crying out at the loss I felt as he did.

My breath caught when he lifted the digits to his mouth and wrapped his lips around them, sucking my pleasure off.

If I hadn't been so damn sated, the action alone would've turned me on. As it was, even the glow around both of us seemed to have vanished.

"I should shower," I managed to say.

"I'll clean you," he said.

My gaze flicked to his bath, and his eyes followed. "Do you want to bathe?"

"I love bathtubs," I admitted. "It's been ages since I soaked."

He scooped me up off the counter, and a squeak escaped me as my core met his naked abdomen. "A bath it is."

Amarok kicked his shorts off as he walked us over to the tub, and held me to his chest as he sank into the water.

My eyes fluttered closed at the blissful heat, and a long groan escaped me as I relaxed into the water. My body was all but glued to his, but neither of us was in a hurry to change that. The physical contact felt too good to bother.

"Thank you," I said, resting my cheek against his chest.

"You shouldn't thank me for pleasuring you," he said, his fingers slipping into my hair and toying with the short strands again. "But you're welcome. Thank you, as well."

"I had fun," I admitted.

"So did I."

My lips curved upward, just the tiniest bit. "I didn't know sex could be like that. So... easy. That's probably a terrible thing to say, though."

"It's not a terrible thing to say. Sex should be fun and relaxing. I'm glad it was almost as enjoyable for you as it was for me."

"You got me off way more than I got you off, so if one of us enjoyed it more, it was definitely me."

He chuckled, his chest rumbling against my body and making me smile again. "Aurora, I took far more pleasure in seeing you bare and making you unravel than I did in my own release. If it's a competition, I've certainly won."

My smile widened. "That's ridiculous."

"Ridiculous, but true." His hand slid out of my hair, and started moving slowly over my back. "You were perfect."

"So were you."

His lips brushed the claim marking on my shoulder. "Feel free to ask me to bring you pleasure at any time. I'll never refuse."

"I don't think I'm very good at realizing when I want things, or what I want. So, don't be offended if I don't ask you."

"I won't feel offense. But I do think many things will change for you now that you're free."

He wasn't wrong.

So many things had *already* changed.

And I was coming around to those changes so much faster than I would've expected.

twelve

RORY

"I CAME HERE to ask what we should do about your pack," I said, a few minutes later. "Kyla told me about the glowing, and said she didn't think your packmates would give us time to figure things out if there was no sign of me glowing."

"If you resisted the frenzy so completely over multiple weeks, and we didn't spend the eclipse together, there is a good chance a few of them would try convincing you to consider them. The frenzy grows stronger the longer it's ignored, however, so I didn't think you'd make it that long without glowing at least a little."

Huh.

Obviously, there was a lot I still didn't know.

"It grows stronger?"

He made a noise of agreement. "Do you see how faint it is around us now?"

I looked at both of us, and realized we *were* still glowing; we just weren't glowing brightly.

"Yes."

"It grows brighter as days pass without satisfying it. Bringing each other sexual release calms it temporarily, but the only way to truly end it is to seal the mate bond."

"Or to let the bond break with the eclipse?" I checked.

"Yes. But if you run from me after the bond is broken, it will likely reignite my mate run."

My eyebrows shot upward. "Run from you?"

"Yes, *physically* run."

"Like a game of tag?"

"I haven't heard of this game."

Right.

"A bunch of people run, and one person chases them, trying to tag them."

"Then yes, like a game of tag. But when you run, it forces my frenzy's magic to the surface, and I have no choice but to chase you. When I catch you, the magic doesn't relent until I've marked you as mine, beginning the bond again and igniting your frenzy as well, assuming you're still attracted to me."

Damn.

"I don't think the attraction is going anywhere now. It's not like I can forget that." I gestured to the bathroom's counter, and his chest rumbled in satisfaction. "But I'll be careful not to run from you."

"It will be easier said than done, soon. You'll begin to itch with the need to shift, and it will drive you to madness if you ignore it." His hands continued to move over my back, calming me.

"Well, that's terrible news."

He chuckled. "You'll enjoy being a wolf, Aurora. The power and freedom you will feel is unmatchable."

My lips curved upward. "You know me too well already."

"I've waited far too long for you not to pay attention when you act and speak."

"I guess that's a valid point." I let out a long breath. "Will my glowing keep the other guys from trying to flirt with me? Your possessiveness will get bad if they do, won't it?"

"I hope it does," he said. "And if it doesn't, we'll deal with it then."

"What about your possessiveness?"

"As long as you don't let my packmates touch you, I'll manage it."

I scowled.

His chest rumbled in soft amusement. "You can always start sleeping in my den. Even my most hard-headed packmates couldn't ignore that as a statement of who you've chosen, with or without a mate bond."

"Do the unmated ladies sleep in their boyfriends' dens?"

"All except Kyla," he said.

"Which is why Kyla has multiple guys chasing her?"

"Yes."

My face warmed as I remembered my thoughts earlier. "Did you ever chase any of the other women?"

"No. I was in the Woods, remember? Waiting for you." His fingers slid up into the soft strands of my hair, and my eyes closed at the comfort of his touch.

"Right."

My mind wandered as peaceful silence filled the room, our bodies entirely relaxed against each other.

Eventually, I decided not to hold back the question I'd been considering. "What would happen if I decided I wasn't interested in mating with you?"

A moment of silence passed.

A long, long moment.

"I would respect your decision, though I would do everything in my power to convince you otherwise."

"Unless I mated with someone else?"

Another silence followed before he admitted, "If you mated with one of my packmates, I would likely lose my battle to immis. I don't tell you that in an attempt to manipulate you or force your hand, but in an effort to be honest. You wouldn't be at fault; I've been waiting to find my fated mate for a long time. Finding her and losing her would be my end."

The peace I'd been feeling slowly faded. I was still relaxed, but nothing was as settled as I had started to feel. Not even a little.

"This is everything to you," I said quietly.

"It is."

Though what he'd said was a little alarming, my mind wasn't going toward red flags, fear, or anything similar.

He was telling me the truth. A truth that would've been a clear signal to run on Earth, but one that was simply a part of living in Evare. The wolves had been struggling with immis for a long time before humans joined them; it wasn't my fault, and he wasn't begging me not to leave him so that he could stay alive.

He was just being honest.

And I appreciated that, tremendously.

"What was mating like, before?" I asked.

"When there were still female shifters?"

I nodded.

"There were so many of us, we didn't feel as much like a family. A male's mate run would begin, and it would often take him to a woman he had never met. He would find her and bite her, she would bite him back immediately, and they would make love then and there. Afterward, they would run until they were ready to settle into her den together. Mating wasn't a choice; it was simply a matter of nature."

"Damn."

He made a noise of agreement. "It took them time to get to know each other, of course. Love was never expected in the beginning. Instead, it was developed over time. From my understanding, that's why the other females in the pack consider fated mates to be an arranged marriage of sorts."

"It's not very romantic," I said, my voice thoughtful.

"It's not about romance. It's about tying two souls and building a bond that will last. That's why some mated couples never progress past friendship. Having honest conversations matters more in the long run than kissing beneath the stars."

My lips curved upward. "I don't know, kissing beneath the stars sounds like fun."

"It does. Although right now, the bathroom countertop sounds like far more fun."

I laughed, lifting my head and meeting his eyes. The small grin he wore was somewhere between mischievous and just genuinely happy.

"So, what are we?" I asked him, still smiling a little. "I have to know how I'm supposed to think about you, and us."

"If I remember correctly, there's a step between dating and married for humans."

"Engaged," I agreed.

"Consider us engaged then, until you decide you're ready to seal the bond." His fingers caught my chin, tilting my head up a little so he could see my eyes better. "I'm ready now, if I haven't made that clear."

"You have, and I think I can work with engaged."

"Good." He brushed his lips against mine. "You make the rules, Aurora. You set the pace, and you determine when and how we progress. Knowing your past, I will never push you."

My throat swelled. "Thank you."

He made a face.

Another laugh escaped me. "You'll have to get used to me thanking you, Amarok."

"Maybe I'll come around to it eventually." He released my chin, but I didn't move my face.

My mouth was ridiculously close to his, and I kind of wanted to kiss him. "Maybe. Or maybe, I can think of a better way to thank you."

His eyes gleamed wickedly. "I like that plan much better."

"I'll see what I can come up with," I lied.

Kissing was what I had come up with.

A lot of kissing, instead of thanking.

But I was nervous to say that, especially after everything we'd done on the countertop. It seemed like a lot of steps forward at once. And while I didn't regret what we'd done at all, and really liked the way it had relaxed things between us, I was still hesitant to commit any more than I already had.

"Why does everyone else call you Rok?" I changed the subject so I wouldn't have to bring up the kissing thing.

He lifted a shoulder. "It was my nickname as a kid, and it stuck."

"If everyone calls you that, why didn't you introduce your-self to me that way?"

"Because you're not everyone else." His hands continued moving on my back. His words and his touch warmed me. "You can call me whatever you want, but to me, names are important. You're my mate. You deserve my full name."

"Is that why you call me Aurora? No one's ever called me that before, by the way."

"It is."

He thought using our whole names was special.

That was... kind of sweet.

"Alright, Amarok it is."

His lips brushed my shoulder, where his claim mark lingered. "I should clean you."

"I think I can handle cleaning myself," I teased him.

"Let me rephrase that: I'm excited to feel your soft skin beneath my hands as I clean you, Aurora."

My lips curved upward. "Guess I can't protest that."

"I hope not." He kissed the claim mark again. "Let me grab the soap."

My eyes closed as his slick hands moved over my back a moment later, sliding up to my shoulders before he eased me away from his chest. His gaze was hot as it moved slowly down to my breasts, and his chest rumbled with satisfaction.

His hands moved slowly down my arms and back up before they slid over my collarbone and caught my breasts.

"Veil, I could touch you forever." His gaze smoldered as he dragged his thumbs over my nipples.

My eyes closed. "I wouldn't complain."

He kneaded them for a few long, blissful minutes before his hands slid down and slowly moved over my folds, lingering on my clit long enough to make me warm.

"I'm never going to be able to leave your den at this rate," I whispered. His soapy hands found my legs and slowly stroked down the length of one of them.

"Then I'm succeeding, I'd say."

I tried to bite my lip to hide my smile, but failed. "I have to agree."

Amarok nipped at my throat. "After I've cleaned you, I'll let you go if you want me to."

I wouldn't want him to... but I'd force myself to go anyway. I could never let myself end up in another mess like the last one I'd been in.

I needed time to establish myself in Evare and make sure I had what I needed, regardless of how good Amarok could make me feel.

He could be the best man in two worlds, and I would still need to find myself before I could let him truly make me his.

thirteen

AMAROK

RORY TOOK my hand and let me help her out of my den, dressed in my shirt instead of her own. Her bodysuit had gone back on, but it didn't have nearly as much hair on it as her shirt had.

She flashed me a smile as she straightened and looked around.

Veil, the light in her eyes made me really damn certain fate had chosen correctly.

"Thanks for the haircut, and everything else."

"Any time." I lifted her hand to my lips, pressing a kiss to the backs of her fingers.

"Would you mind helping me find the other women? I think Ezra said something about a shop they were working on."

"Of course." I released her hand, and after a moment's hesitation, she wrapped it around my arm and stepped up to my side.

Pride swelled in my chest as we walked through the pack's land, neither of us in a hurry. "What did you like to do on Earth?"

"It's been a long time since I've had a hobby," she admitted. "Keeping Allen from losing his shit felt like a second full-time job, and I worked sixty hours at the hospital every week just to stay away from him. So, there wasn't time for anything else. When I really needed a break, I liked to go for walks outside. The fresh air always felt good, and helped me think more clearly."

I nodded. "You'll like running in your wolf form, then."

"I hope so." She gave me another smile, her expression much lighter and happier than it had been before she let me pleasure her. Though I wouldn't say it aloud, I was certain my attention had lifted her spirit and made her a little more comfortable in Evare.

Veil, I hoped she'd let me continue to take care of her that way.

"What do you do for fun?" she asked me.

"Fun has been relative for a long time. All of my energy went into keeping the pack together before Serae brought Ezra here. After the first two women arrived without warning, I moved to the Woods and spent all my time there."

"So we're both terrible at having fun."

"Sounds like it," I agreed, my lips curving slightly.

"We'll have to fix that. I'll ask the other girls what there is to do for fun here, and then we can make a list."

My lips curved further. "Alright."

"You'll do the things with me, even if they're weird?" she checked, looking over at me.

"Not much is weird when you're an ancient shifter, Aurora."

She smiled. "Good point. What is this shop they're working on?"

I gave her a quick description of the place that would be the grocery store, and what the other women were doing. We had tried to keep them out of our construction efforts at first, but Ezra said they needed something to focus on, so we'd backed off. Now, Ezra and Ivaylo worked with which-ever women wanted to be involved on the interior, including polishing the stone, building the furniture, and decorating.

We hadn't bothered decorating much in centuries, so that bit was the strangest for us males.

Aurora grew excited when I explained the project, and by the time we reached the shop, she was nearly bouncing with energy. Ezra, Ivaylo, Riley, and Jill were all working inside, with Ivaylo giving the instructions.

The other men and I knew how completely obsessed our alpha was with his mate. We'd seen then together long enough that having him around our females didn't worry any of us.

"Hey, Rory!" Ezra flashed her a grin, and the other women did too. "You look better."

"Amarok fixed my hair." She fluffed the damp strands with her hand, and Ezra's grin widened.

"That's not what I was talking about, but it looks good too."

My mate's face flushed, and I ran my hand over hers, where she rested it on my arm. "I'll be outside if you need me. We're clearing out another den right now."

She nodded, her cheeks still red. "Thanks."

As much as it pained me to do so, I forced myself to stride out of the building as if I wasn't worried about leaving her.

My female needed time and space. She needed to be certain that I didn't want to control her the way Allen had—that her freedom meant as much to me as it did to her.

"Damn, he walked away much easier than I would've expected," Ezra remarked.

"He knows it's not going to work out between us if he can't," Aurora admitted, her voice growing fainter in my ears as the distance between us increased. "He doesn't want to leave me, but I need him to, and he understands that."

I walked a bit taller with her words in my mind, and forced myself to focus as much as possible while I was away from her.

She needed space—and I would give her what she needed, even if it killed me.

fourteen

RORY

I LOVED WORKING in the shop. It was fun chatting with the other girls, and they filled in the gaps between what I knew and didn't know about Evare. For the most part, I understood everything, but there were a few things I hadn't quite wrapped my mind around.

The eclipse was still one of those things. The grins they wore when they told me it was something I just had to experience for myself reassured me that I didn't need to worry about it.

I ate dinner with the pack in the massive den after the suns went down that day, and it was surreal. I still leaned heavily against Amarok when the other werewolf guys were around —Ezra told me they didn't care if we called them shifters or werewolves—but I couldn't expect myself to adjust to the sheer size of them overnight.

My past was still my past, after all.

And I felt safe enough tucked against Amarok's side that I didn't worry about any of them, so it wasn't a big deal.

He walked me back to my den afterward, and I was exhausted enough that I just gave him a quick hug before climbing back into my space and collapsing on my bed.

WHEN THE NEXT morning came around, I showered and got dressed before climbing outside. I stared at a big, furry beast I found out there for a moment, before I realized Amarok had slept outside my den again, in his wolf form.

My guilt must've shown on my face, because he murmured into my mind, *"I stayed here because I chose to, Aurora. Not because I had to. I want you to be comfortable in your own space, not to adapt for me because of guilt."*

His words didn't wipe away my feelings, but they did ease them.

I satisfied them the rest of the way by letting him make me breakfast in his den, like he wanted to, then forcing him to take a shower before we left again. He acted grumbly about it, but I could tell he liked that I was making him take care of himself.

Nothing steamy happened, and we spent the day working peacefully with the pack before eating dinner with everyone, like we had the night before.

We fell into a pattern, and the days passed quickly. Breakfast in Amarok's den, both of us ignoring the lust that literally glowed around us, a full day of work, and then a hug at the opening of my den before we spent the night separately.

It wasn't everything I wanted, but it felt necessary. I had to give myself time to process and adjust, after all.

And honestly, I was happy with it.

So ridiculously happy, I could hardly believe it.

I woke up with a smile on my face in the mornings, and greeted Amarok with enough enthusiasm that it made him smile too. His smiles felt even better to me than my own, somehow.

TWO AND A HALF weeks flew by quickly, and then we were finally walking back toward my den the night before the eclipse.

Our movements were slower than usual, and my hand was tucked in the crook of his elbow, our sides brushing with every few steps.

We hadn't discussed the eclipse. As Amarok had promised, he hadn't asked me for or pushed me on a single thing. I set the pace, and he followed my lead exactly.

"So…" I trailed off, as we neared my den.

He was quiet, but when I glanced at him, I didn't see any concerning emotions on his face or in his posture. He still looked about as relaxed as I could've expected him to be.

"What will happen here, tomorrow?" I gestured to the pack's land around us.

"Nothing. Everyone will stay secluded in their dens, and we built them deep enough that sound doesn't escape them."

That was a relief, I supposed.

All of the other women were spending the eclipse with their mates or boyfriends—even Kyla, who had tentatively agreed to steadily date a lonely werewolf named Worren.

I hadn't come out and told Amarok that I planned on spending the day with him. I'd suggested it that day we touched each other in his bathroom, but it had never been decided for sure.

He wouldn't ask me, but I could imagine how the day would go if I didn't spend it with him. He wouldn't leave me unguarded, so he'd spend it out in the open, which I would never let happen.

So, I needed to breach the subject we hadn't dared touch.

We walked a few more minutes before we were too close to my den to avoid the question any longer.

"Do you still want to spend the eclipse with me?" I blurted.

"Of course." He lifted his free hand to rest on mine, sandwiching it between his arm and palm. "But I'm content to guard your home if you aren't comfortable with it."

I wasn't anywhere near uncomfortable with it.

Most evenings, I went to bed imagining what it would be like if I'd managed to gather the guts to go home with Amarok, even if I knew I should take the time to heal.

I didn't feel broken.

I didn't feel trapped anymore, or lost.

Then again, I had emotionally disengaged from my relationship with Allen the first time I'd tried to run away from him, which was over a year before Serae brought me to Evare. So... yeah.

I wanted Amarok.

Did that mean I was going to let myself get lost in him, or blinded by my desire?

No, it did not.

But it also didn't mean I was going to make both of us spend the eclipse miserable. We *could* enjoy ourselves together. And from what I'd heard, it could be *very* enjoyable.

"I'm confident you'll make me more comfortable than I have any right to be," I told him, earning a slow, panty-melting grin from the shifter.

"In that case, we need to walk this way." He turned me around with a soft tug, making me laugh as I bumped into him, which he had clearly intended.

Our sides brushed with every step we took, and my smile was so wide, I couldn't have fought it if I tried.

"When will the claim mark vanish?" I asked him, as we neared his den.

Despite the question, his grin remained in place. "Sometime in the middle of the night, I'd imagine. Around the same time the lust hits."

The glow around me swelled at the mention of lust, and Amarok's pulsed alongside mine.

We didn't bring up our frenzy's reactions as I climbed down, followed by Amarok.

He pulled the lever to lock the den behind us, and I turned to face him, studying him. Despite the darkness, I had no problem making out every inch of him. My transition to a shifter had ended a while ago, though I still hadn't shifted. I'd started to feel a bit of an urge to run, which the other women told me was a sign that I could shift, whenever I decided to.

I just hadn't decided to yet.

Eventually, the urge that they called the "itch" would get too strong to ignore. Then, I'd have no choice.

But for the moment, it was nothing more than a small annoyance.

Amarok's eyes moved over my figure, hot and slow, and heat blossomed on my cheeks.

The wetness between my thighs was obnoxious, but I wasn't about to jump him. We'd spend all day in bed when the morning came around, after all.

"Want to make dessert? Ezra taught me how to make those things you guys all love. What are they called again?"

"Hmm?" He lifted his gaze to mine, the glow around him pulsing brighter than I'd ever seen it except that day in the bathroom.

"Dessert?" I repeated.

"Sounds good." His murmur made goosebumps break out on my skin, but I ignored them, strolling into the kitchen like my heart wasn't thumping hard in my chest.

His hand brushed my hip, the touch innocent, but enough to make the frenzy's need swell hotter around me and within me.

Shit, I wanted him.

"Where's your recipe book?" I asked.

He pulled it from a cupboard rather than answering me.

And instead of giving it to me, he set it down on the countertop beside me and opened it up. His hand slid over my hip again, his front brushing my back lightly. "What do you want?"

I bit my tongue to stop myself from saying, "You."

"Something with chocolate," I managed, after a moment.

I had been planning to make dessert for him, but that plan was out the window.

"You sit. I'll cook."

"You don't have any chairs," I reminded him, still facing away. "And I—oof!" My ass landed on the counter, and my eyes met his. With that added height, our gazes were level.

"I like taking care of you, Aurora. Just sit here and talk to me while I bake for you."

Damn.

Could he have said something sexier, if he tried?

I didn't think so.

"A conversation doesn't seem like a fair trade," I finally protested, when he looked down at the recipe long enough to start pulling ingredients from the pantry and fridge (they called them iceboxes in Evare, but all of us women stuck with fridge).

"If you want to feel more equal, you could take your clothes off. Letting me talk to you *and* look at you while I cook would be more than fair."

I snorted, and he flashed me a grin.

His glow was still insanely bright, but it was no longer pulsing. It had settled on a steady, vibrant golden light.

Mine had mostly settled too, and was almost as bright as his.

My gaze flicked to his shorts, and my face flushed at the sight of the tent in the fabric.

I wanted to touch him.

So much for my glow being steady. It had started bouncing and pulsing again.

Amarok's attention was on the recipe for the moment, so I decided to take him up on his offer.

Nudity in exchange for cooking.

It was a good deal, considering the man I was acting as eye-candy for.

His gaze was hot on my figure as I pulled my shirt over my head, exposing the thin bodysuit beneath. It didn't show anything, but it clung to me like a second skin.

Though he didn't say a word, the glow around him lost its steadiness the same way my own had. It pulsed brightly, and his hand slid over my thigh as he forced his attention back to the recipe book.

His fingers stroked the inside of my leg as he read, and I leaned my head back against the cabinets, watching him touch me.

Did I want him to touch more of me?

Yes, I most definitely did.

And unfortunately, I was going to have to be the one to start it. He had made it clear that he wasn't going to instigate anything.

Thankfully, my horniness made me brave.

When he released my leg to grab a few more things, I slipped out of my bodysuit.

Amarok's gaze jerked back to me, and his eyes blazed over my skin while his chest rumbled fiercely.

"Can you cook with one hand?" I asked him, a bit breathlessly.

"No. Touch yourself for me."

"Ezra told me you can't get yourself off during the frenzy."

"Not alone," he agreed. "But you're not alone, are you?"

Ohhh.

It had been years since I dared... but I wanted to.

I really, really did.

Biting my lip, I slipped my fingers between my thighs.

Amarok's growl mingled with my soft groan, and both reverberated through the den as I parted my legs wider, stroking myself lightly.

"Veil, you're the sexiest thing I've ever seen. Make yourself climax for me." Amarok's hand brushed my thigh again, opening me wider so he could see everything while we both worked.

That was the kind of order I could get behind from a man.

I touched myself while he added ingredients, then as he mixed the dough and watched me with hooded eyes. Just as he closed the Evare version of an oven, I finally lost control.

My cries flooded the den as my hips jerked on the counter-top. Pleasure rolled through me, and the satisfaction in his eyes was so thick I could see it.

He set his hands on my thighs again, gripping me lightly while I came down from the high.

"How do you feel, Aurora?"

"So good," I breathed, my chest still rising and falling quickly. One of my hands was still resting over my core, and the other gripped the countertop like a lifeline. My cheeks were probably bright red, but he only touched them long enough to tuck a few stray strands of hair behind my ear.

I didn't say a word as he took my hand from between my thighs and slowly lifted it to his mouth.

Or as he wrapped his lips around my fingers and slowly sucked the slickness off my skin.

My breathing grew shallower, the frenzy still pulsing around both of us. From experience, I knew the glow wouldn't vanish unless we were both sated.

"How much control will we lose during the eclipse?" I asked him breathlessly.

"Almost all of it."

"So you think we'll have full-out sex?"

His chest rumbled. "Without a doubt."

"There's no point in waiting then, is there?"

"Not to me."

Good.

That was really, really good.

I brushed my knee against his erection, making his chest rumble again, much more fiercely. "Maybe we should try out your bed, then."

A soft squeal escaped me as he grabbed my thighs, striding across the room while I held onto his shoulders for dear life.

fifteen

RORY

MY GAZE LINGERED on Amarok's mouth, and my mind went back to what I'd been itching to do since that day in the bathroom.

To kiss him.

If we were going to spend the eclipse with his cock buried inside me, there was no point in being shy about it. It would be better to start from the bottom anyway, wouldn't it?

Though my uncertainty was thick, I wasn't the same scared, trapped woman I'd been on Earth. I was free now, and what was the worst that could happen? He wouldn't like it, and would refuse to kiss me again?

Amarok set me on the edge of the bed, and started to let go of me.

He was going to lick me; I knew it without asking.

And I wanted that—shit, I wanted that.

But I wanted to make it clear to him that our relationship wasn't one-sided. Even if it was just friendship that had gotten a little physical because of an impending solar event, it wasn't just him.

"Wait," I whispered, grabbing his face in my hands.

His eyes were hot, but his movements stilled at my words, his body leaning over mine and his hands still trapped beneath my thighs.

Instead of telling him what I wanted, I forced my hesitation aside, leaned in, and kissed him.

His chest rumbled again as our lips touched—and a groan escaped him when I slipped my tongue into his mouth. A heartbeat later, his tongue was moving with mine, the motions slow, sexy, and explorative.

My fingers slipped into his thick, soft curls, digging into the strands. His hands left my thighs as he lowered my back to the mattress. We were both sprawled over it, our legs hanging off the ledge as we kissed.

And kissed.

And kissed.

The heat of our frenzy grew more frantic as the kiss went on, until I was pulsing with overwhelming desire.

I wanted him.

No, I *needed* him.

But he didn't want me to say that—he wanted me to take charge.

To show him what I wanted.

So, dizzy with lust, I slipped my hands out of his hair and moved them down the gorgeous expanse of his back. The waistband of his shorts molded to my fingers before I managed to push them down.

And down.

And down.

My breath caught as the thick heat of his cock sprung free, nestling between my thighs. The head of him brushed my clit as he throbbed, and a low growl vibrated his chest against me as he kept kissing me.

I still wanted him.

I still *needed* him.

And he was mine.

My hands found his hair again, and I tugged on the strands. He moved up a little at my request, and the head of his cock pressed lightly against my core.

I arched my hips just enough, and he found the slickness of my entrance.

His soft snarl pulled his mouth away from mine, and I took him back.

I wanted his tongue moving with mine while he filled me. The kiss was relaxing me, making the moment so much more exciting, and keeping my bad memories at bay. I wasn't willing to risk changing that, not the first time we had sex.

So I kissed him, and damn, he kissed me back.

His tongue's movements grew more demanding, his body remaining still as he waited for me to be ready.

I hooked a leg around his ass, and lifted my hips again, taking him deeper.

When I sucked in a breath at the sudden fullness, he kissed me harder, swearing into my mind, *"Fuck, Aurora. You feel unbelievable."*

The compliment made me even hotter, and I hooked my other leg around his ass, lifting my hips again. He thrust to meet me, and we groaned together when he bottomed out inside me.

I had never imagined I could feel so full.

He was massive—absolutely massive—and shit, just having him inside me was so much more pleasurable than I would have ever thought.

His hands found my ass, and he lifted me more as he slowly started to move. My body met his stroke for stroke, and our kiss went on.

Our motions grew more and more desperate. When he finally worked a finger between out bodies and dragged his thumb over my clit, just that one touch was enough to set me off.

I screamed as I unraveled, my hands yanking his hair and my hips bucking violently as I chased the pleasure. Amarok snarled with me, his cock dragging out my pleasure as he flooded me with his release.

"Holy shit," I panted, my hips still jerking a little as I came down from the high. His forehead rested against mine, his lips finally giving my own a break. "I've never had an orgasm like *that* before."

"That makes two of us," he growled, his breaths heavy against my mouth. His cock was still throbbing lightly inside me, and my channel felt warmer and slicker than ever before.

"I didn't think you'd feel so good," I admitted, forcing myself to loosen my grip on his hair.

"I'll take that as a compliment."

A soft laugh escaped me. "You should." I kept my legs wrapped tightly around his backside, not wanting him to pull away. "Can you roll us over?"

He made a noise of agreement, kicked his shorts the rest of the way off, and rolled us. I sucked in a breath at the sudden change in feeling with that position. "Ezra and the other girls told me werewolf men don't need breaks between orgasms like human guys," I managed to say.

"We don't." His hands pulled my legs out from under him, and then found my ass, massaging it slowly. "You look incredible with my release spilling out of you like this, Aurora."

A shiver rolled through me, and I looked down. My gaze caught on the place we connected, with his cock stretching me open. The evidence of both of our pleasure coated the base of his cock and the apex of my thighs, and the sight of it made me tense around him.

He growled, squeezing my ass in response to my tenseness. "I don't have the words to describe how good you feel."

"Neither do I." I planted my hands on his abdomen and leaned over him.

One of his hands released my ass and slid around to the front of me. When his thumb brushed my clit, I cried out, bucking against him.

The feeling was so good, I chased it, moving faster and harder on his cock. The sounds he made and the way he touched me told me he had no problem with me using him —and we shattered together again soon enough.

His eyes were still molten when they moved over my naked figure while we came down from the high.

"I should be tired of this by now," I said, pushing sweaty strands of hair out of my eyes and tucking them behind my ear.

"I'm really damn glad you're not." Amarok held my hips in place and slowly thrust in and out. It shouldn't have felt so good—but holy hell, it did.

"We should save some of our energy for tomorrow," I told him weakly, after we climaxed together for the third time.

"We can if you want," he agreed, his fingers stilling temporarily on my clit.

"After this," I finally said, controlling the pace again as I moved on his cock.

The words were a lie.

I didn't want to stop after that.

But as we lost control, a timer started to buzz. Amarok growled as I collapsed on his chest, exhausted and blissed-out beyond my wildest dreams.

He rolled me to my back, easing out of me slowly, but I still made a noise of protest at the loss of him.

Amarok captured my mouth, giving me a soft, lingering kiss before he pulled away. "I'll be back with chocolate."

I groaned.

Chocolate sounded *so* good.

His lips curved upward, and he brushed another kiss to my mouth before he strode across the room. I couldn't stop myself from watching that gorgeous, inked-up ass walk away from me—and even if I could've, I wouldn't have.

Because he was mine, even if I wasn't ready to accept every aspect of the mating bond.

My gaze lingered on him as he pulled a pan of what almost resembled cookies from the oven, and then drizzled some kind of glaze over them.

A few minutes later, he was walking back across the room with a plate of them in his hand. His cock was still rock hard, and damp with our pleasure. My face flushed at the sight of him, and the cookies were a forgotten notion.

"I want you," I whispered to him, as he sat down beside me.

"Good. You can have me, as soon as you've cleaned the plate." He dragged a finger through a small puddle of the icing, and lifted it to my mouth. I didn't hesitate to take it between my lips, and his chest rumbled in satisfaction when I groaned at the sweet, chocolatey taste.

"You're going to force me to eat dessert?" I released his finger, my voice a little playful.

"Mmhm. Open." He lifted the cookie to my mouth, and I took a dutiful bite.

Another groan escaped me, and I said with a full mouth, "Holy shit." It came out more like "hooy shiih" and his eyes flooded with satisfaction.

I swallowed the bite. "Those are *so* good, thank you."

He bopped me on the tip of my nose with the cookie. "No more thanking me."

"I can't help it," I protested, taking another bite when he offered it. After I'd swallowed, I added, "And I can feed myself."

"Alright." He leaned in and licked the frosting off my nose. I plucked the cookie from his hand, and took a bite.

His gaze grew a little wicked as he looked down at the icing. "Can I touch you while you eat?"

My mouth was full, so I nodded.

He dipped his finger in the chocolate glaze, and then lowered it to my nipple, slowly drawing a floral shape around it.

Amusement flooded me, and I shook my head at him, but continued eating.

His lips stretched in a wicked grin as he continued painting me with the icing while I ate, covering my breasts and abdomen with flowery shapes and swirls. If my core hadn't been so slick with both our releases, I was sure he'd have painted that too.

By the time I finished the dessert, my body was a damn masterpiece.

"What am I supposed to do now?" I teased him, knowing damn well how he intended to clean me up.

"Just slip your hands into my hair and stay where you are." He lowered himself between my legs and slowly dragged the tip of his tongue over the first of the lines, just above my core.

The warm slickness shocked me so much I nearly arched off the bed, and he had only licked my *belly*.

"Wow," I choked out.

"You're delicious," he murmured against my abdomen, following another line down toward my core.

My hips moved a little, and one of his hands landed on my thigh, holding it in place.

His tongue slid back up my abdomen, and continued slowly cleaning the icing off my body.

I was a puddle of hot, desperate need by the time his mouth reached my breasts, and his thumb brushed my clit.

My body practically *writhed* under the intense heat of that touch, but he didn't give me more.

He tasted and teased my soft, sensitive flesh, only giving my clit the softest of brushes.

Finally, his tongue followed the last line of icing down to my core.

My cries echoed in the den as he ate me out, shattering me far too soon—and then filling me with his cock again until we both lost ourselves to even more pleasure.

After we came down from the high, he carried me to the bathroom. He cleaned me up in the tub with soft, gentle hands that made me like him even more.

When we curled up in bed together, I let myself imagine just for a moment, that I could spend every night tucked against his side and feeling like the luckiest woman in the world.

I couldn't let myself believe my future would truly look like that... but I couldn't stop myself from hoping for it, either.

RORY

LUST WOKE us both early the next morning, and Amarok didn't waste any time before burying his face between my thighs and making me cry out again. My consciousness faded as he made love to me with his mouth, and I was reduced to little more than a desperate animal as the lust grew even stronger.

We had sex everywhere.

So damn much sex.

In the bed.

In the bath.

In the shower.

On the bathroom countertop again.

In the kitchen.

He hadn't been kidding when he said we'd have almost no control over ourselves; we were both lost entirely to the eclipse.

When the need and pleasure finally faded, I was exhausted. I dropped my head to Amarok's shoulder and let out a long, content sigh. "Wow."

"Finally, I understand why mated couples enjoy eclipses," he murmured against my face, sliding out of me and lifting me higher in his arms.

"That was…" I trailed off, having no words for it.

He walked us to the bathroom and slipped into the tub, holding me to his chest. "Mmhm."

"Yeah." I closed my eyes and let out a long, contented sigh as the warm water covered me to my chin. "How am I not sore?"

"You're a shifter, Aurora. We heal much faster than humans, and are much harder to injure." He grabbed the soap and cleaned me slowly, not minding at all that I was nearly boneless with exhaustion and pleasure. "You should be hungry, though. I'll make you something to eat as soon as you're clean and dry."

My stomach rumbled as if in agreement, and I couldn't stop myself from smiling.

It had been a good day.

A really, really good day.

And it was going to be a good night, too.

. . .

SOON ENOUGH, I was clean and tucked into Amarok's bed wearing one of his shirts. My hair was still a little damp, but drying quickly, and I watched him cook. He'd put on shorts, so the sight wasn't as good as it could've been, but I enjoyed it anyway.

As I watched him, I was forced to admit to myself how much I enjoyed being around him. He was a safe man, who respected me and treated me the way I deserved to be treated, and...

Well, I cared about him.

More than I should've, truthfully.

And maybe that should've scared me, but it didn't.

It did make me quiet as we ate and then curled up in bed together though, because the implications of it were huge.

Massively huge.

And despite my feelings, I knew I couldn't let myself face those implications yet.

So, I cuddled up against him and let myself fall asleep in his arms, deciding that I'd figure out what I was going to do about the next day when it finally came, and not a moment before.

WHEN THE MORNING CAME AROUND, it felt surprisingly normal. He made me breakfast, and asked me about what we'd done on the shop since he last looked at it.

Though neither of us brought up the eclipse, or instigated anything sexual, we traded a number of searing looks that neither of us could ignore.

Still, after we ate, we climbed out of his den like we weren't doing the walk of shame. The pack was already up and moving, and I saw a lot more single men around than I expected to.

Amarok stayed closer to me than he ever had before as we walked across the pack's land. His hand brushed my lower back for the dozenth time in five minutes, and realization struck me.

My gaze dropped to my neck, and I found it bare of the mark we'd shared.

The silvery mark had vanished.

Our bond was gone.

Neither of us was glowing at all.

There was no more frenzy, and nothing else pushing us to be together.

My stomach clenched at the idea, though.

I noticed a few guys staring at me, and my eyes widened slightly.

I smelled like Amarok, but other than that, there was absolutely nothing marking me as his, or preventing them from hitting on me.

That was...

It was a lot.

And I wasn't sure what to do or think about it.

"I'll stay close, in case you need me," he murmured before he kissed me lightly, right outside the shop. "Just call my name, and I'll find you."

I nodded, unsure what else I should do or say.

Honestly, I wasn't even sure where we stood.

I was almost positive that in his mind, we were still as close to engaged as you could get in Evare.

But did I feel the same way?

We'd had sex—so much sex.

So much *really great* sex.

And I felt safe with him. I trusted him, which felt pretty massive considering my track record with men.

The only problem was that I didn't really *know* him. I had never made an effort to learn about his past, other than the basics. And I'd never seen him interact with his pack a whole lot, even though they were his whole life. We always stuck to the outer edges at pack dinners, and people gave us space because of our frenzy.

But considering all the eyes on me, things were clearly changing.

Which meant I either needed to decide to get to know Amarok so we could eventually seal a bond, or let him go.

The idea of walking away from him forever made my heart squeeze, and the memory of our conversation about that made my throat swell.

I couldn't let him go. If I did, he would most likely lose himself to immis.

And did I even want to let him go?

Looking into those intense, dark eyes, I realized that even if he didn't lose himself to immis, I still wouldn't want to let go. What if I had to see him kiss another woman?

Shit, the thought made me nauseous.

Was I already possessive of him too?

That possibility scared the hell out of me.

"Are we good?" I asked him, stepping closer so our bodies met. There was clothing between us, obviously, but I needed the physical contact. I set my hands on his chest, too, unable to stop myself.

His arm went around my waist. "We're great, Aurora." His lips caught mine, and his tongue slipped into my mouth, slowly reassuring me with his kiss. My body and mind were much more relaxed when he pulled away a minute later. "We don't need marks to be mates, do we?"

"Not really," I whispered, my palms still pressing against his skin.

"If you're comfortable with it, we'll move your stuff to my den tonight. If not, we'll keep doing what we're doing. You know I don't mind waiting until you're ready."

I nodded, feeling much better about our situation, even though some of it was up in the air.

"Hey, Rory!" Riley caught my elbow and flashed me a grin. "You don't look worse for the wear, at least."

My face flushed, and I couldn't help but laugh. "Neither do you."

"I'll see you at lunch time." Amarok caught my hand and lifted it to his lips, so he could brush a kiss to the backs of my knuckles.

"You'll see her at casino night, you mean," Riley corrected him.

He frowned.

Her grin widened. "Ask some of the guys about it."

With that, she towed me into the shop. I shrugged a shoulder in Amarok's direction as we went, and he gave me a small smile before the door closed behind us.

"What's casino night?" I asked, surprised to see that we were the first ladies in the shop.

"Oh, it's a fun tradition we started after the last eclipse. We all dress up ridiculously and run a huge card game tournament with everyone. The unmated guys eat it up, and love that it means they get to interact with the unmated women more than usual. You'll have everyone's attention, I'm sure."

Oh. "I think I'm still with Amarok."

"You think?" She raised her eyebrows back at me.

"No, I am—we're still together." I stumbled over the words a bit. "I'm just trying to figure out the dynamic."

"Relationships are weird here, but you'll work through it." She squeezed my hand. "And you'll love Casino Night, I promise. The game we play is sort of the Evare version of poker, so you'll be just as much at a disadvantage as the rest of us are. And the guys *don't* go easy on us."

"They're probably competitive," I thought aloud.

"Extremely. We made rules to stop fights from breaking out this time, at least. And hats of punishment."

I snorted. "Hats of punishment?"

Her grin lingered. "You'll see."

I was looking forward to it.

WE WORKED FOR AN HOUR, and then Ezra finally came stumbling in, looking like she hadn't slept a wink. There was a smile on her face though, and a gleam in her eyes I wasn't sure I'd ever had in my own.

"Damn, you guys got back to it quick," she remarked. "Didn't enjoy the eclipse?"

My body warmed at the reminder.

"We enjoyed it, we just also enjoyed our sleep. Unlike you." Riley winked at her.

Ezra laughed. "I slept. Ivaylo woke me up halfway through the night to go for a run, though."

Riley wiggled her eyebrows. "A run?"

"Mmhm. Best run of my life."

Riley snorted. "Every run is the best of your life."

"So, so true."

I frowned. "Why is running sexy?"

The women exchanged knowing looks, and Ezra explained. "The frenzy's magic disappears when you seal the bond, but it doesn't go away entirely. The guys keep it, in here." She tapped on her sternum. "If you run from your mate, it sets off the magic again. Not to the same extent a mate run does, but enough to make their eyes glow gold and turn them into little more than sexy, sexy animals."

My eyes widened. "Shit."

"Yup. It's hot, if you're into that kind of thing. If you're not, don't run." She studied me for a moment. "You're still with Rok, right?"

I nodded. "Yeah, we're still sort of engaged."

"Sort of?" Her eyebrows lifted, just like Riley's had.

"She's still trying to figure out how to do relationships in Evare. They'll get there." Riley patted Ezra on the shoulder. "Let's get a little more work done, so we can get ready for casino night."

"Good idea," Ezra agreed, and we all got back to work.

AT LUNCH TIME, Riley and Ezra dragged me back to the women's den, where we all ate dessert for lunch before we started getting ready for casino night.

Getting ready involved eating snacks and chatting while we used the closest thing Evare had to makeup to stain our lips bright pink. We looked ridiculous, but none of us could stop grinning because of it.

We spent ages debating the brightest-colored shirts, and then selecting from the lovely assortment of hats the women had created.

To finish off the looks, we pulled these huge, weird, fluffy leaves over our shoulders like they were feather boas. Apparently, they grew on a few trees in the far east corner of the pack's land. They were the most similar plant Evare had to a palm tree, as far as Ezra knew.

Anyway, by the time we all left the den together, we looked truly atrocious—and ridiculously happy.

seventeen

AMAROK

VALKO DRAGGED me in for a hug. It had been months since I'd seen him, and damn, it was good to catch up. "You're a mated man now, I hear."

"That's the hope," I agreed.

"Well you stink of a woman, so clearly the hope is working out for you."

My lips stretched in a grin, and I didn't argue with him.

Aurora still seemed a little unsure, but we were getting there, and that was more than enough for me.

"How long before you head out again?" I asked him, as we walked toward the pack's den.

"Kuro should be back tomorrow from the Hills, so I'm replacing him. Most of the other guys don't like being so far from the pack."

"Neither do you," I pointed out.

He shrugged. "It's nice to have a break, at least."

I couldn't argue with that.

We'd been at our wits' end just trying to keep everyone alive, and now, there wasn't a damn thing for us to do except dig dens and patrol different parts of the Woods for new women. It was blissful, compared to what we had been doing.

And having Aurora with me, everything was going to change. I wouldn't be dealing with nearly as much shit alone any longer, thankfully. If there was ever a day I didn't want to deal with the pack, I could just stay home and take care of my mate, without feeling like I was letting anyone down.

"What's your mate like?" he asked me, as we approached the casino.

"Perfect." My chest ached at the reminder of her.

Our breakfasts and hours during the eclipse weren't enough. I needed time to get to know her, and learn to understand her more. What I knew of her barely scratched the surface, and that was nowhere near passable.

I'd been giving her space to wrap her head around everything, but veil, I wanted more.

Valko snorted. "Should've expected that."

"She's small and fragile, but strong-willed and resilient. When she smiles, no one can stop themselves from smiling back. Around her, I feel steady and sure."

Valko whistled. "What's her name?"

"Rory."

"You'll have to introduce me to her," he said.

I couldn't suppress the growl that rose in my throat, and he flashed me a knowing grin. "No completed mate bond?"

"Not yet. We're getting there."

He nodded, and we reached the den.

IT TOOK an hour or two for our handful of men to arrange and decorate the den the way the women had instructed us to. When we were finally done, it was nearly time for the tournament to start.

Brightly colored shorts and fuzzy leaves were passed out. Though I did so a bit disgruntled, I accepted the clothes and changed into them quickly, tossing the long, fluffy red leaf over one shoulder.

Valko threw his own fuzzy leaf back in the pile a few of our other packmates had made, snorting when he saw me. I figured the flamboyant leaf would make Aurora smile, so mine stayed on my shoulder.

Ivaylo walked in dressed in the same brightly-colored shorts Valko and I had on, as well as a large, colorful hat made of a combination of fabric, paint, and leaves.

"The women are excited. Put your damn boas on," the alpha grumbled at all of us, tossing a hand toward the pile of fuzzy leaves.

Apparently, the women called them boas.

The guys, including Valko, made a show of reluctantly throwing the things over one shoulder, like I had.

"You know the rules, bastards. Don't touch the women unless they touch you first, or unless they belong to you." He glanced over at Worren. "Permanently. Unless they belong to you *permanently*."

"Don't look at me. Rok's the one with the uncertain female." Worren tossed a hand in my direction.

"We're fated," I growled back, fists clenching at my sides.

"The rule applies to him too. No mark on your shoulder, no touching the woman unless she touches you first. While this is going on, at least. I don't give a damn what you do after it ends, as long as the women are in favor of it." Ivaylo tossed one end of his boa over his opposite shoulder. "And veil, guys, *ask* before you bring the women food if they haven't requested it."

A few of the men at the back of the group grumbled at that rule. I assumed there was some kind of a story behind it, but wasn't curious enough to ask.

"Just don't do anything that would piss off your future mate if she finds out about it," the alpha finally said. "Now, act like I haven't just lectured you. Ezra will bring the women in soon."

A few chuckles went through the group, and everyone spread out, making themselves comfortable. Some took seats at the tables we set up and started a game of cards, while a few others got to work in the kitchen.

Ivaylo strode over to me and Valko, and said in a low voice, "Sorry, Rok. You know I favor fate, but the last thing we need is to start a riot over who's allowed to touch an unclaimed woman. I'm sure your female will come straight to you, anyway."

Veil, I hoped so.

I lifted a shoulder in a shrug. "I would've made the same announcement."

"Us horny unmated males need rules, after all," Valko drawled, earning a snort from Ivaylo and a grin from me.

"You'll find your female soon enough," Ivaylo said, smacking him on the arm.

"She'll be worth the wait," I added.

Ivaylo's grin widened. "Or she'll be a pain in your ass that you simply wouldn't be willing to live without."

Valko adjusted the furry boa on his shoulder. "That sounds more likely, with my luck."

All of us turned our heads when Ezra called out behind us, "Welcome to Casino Night!" Her arms were spread wide, and she was clearly talking to the women with her. Three of them hadn't been there during the last casino night, including Aurora, and looked around with smiles on their faces.

My gaze moved slowly down my mate's body. She had on a bright pink shirt and brighter pink boa, with her lips stained the same color. I knew she'd chosen it to match her hair, and loved the way her entire face lit up with her smile. The odd hat on her head was a mess of different pink shades as well, and only succeeded at making her look even more adorable.

Her gaze caught on mine, and her smile stretched wider, her face pinkening to match the rest of her a little better.

Veil, she was stunning.

And *mine*.

"Find a seat!" Ezra commanded. "One woman at each table to start off with. If you don't know how the tournament works, the guys will teach you."

The girls split up, and I strode across the room. Two bastards had already claimed the seats on either side of Aurora by the time I reached her table, but her smile was so damn huge, I couldn't toss one of them out.

Settling down across the table from her, I listened to Ev explain the rules of the game. It annoyed me that I couldn't speak into Rory's mind any longer, but I knew I needed to keep that feeling capped.

Allen had treated her terribly when she was even slightly friendly to other men, so I had to show her I could keep my emotions in check. The possessiveness, in particular.

That would've been easier if she was sitting on my lap, of course, but I could still smell my scent intertwined with hers. And if I could smell it, everyone else at the table certainly could as well.

Her foot brushed my leg beneath the table once, as she asked questions about the instructions. I didn't think much of it.

When it brushed my calf again, more slowly, her eyes met mine and she flashed me a small grin.

The lingering annoyance I'd carried faded, and I mirrored the expression.

She was still mine, and we both knew it.

The game began, and we all played our cards a few times.

Two of the guys were out after the first round, one of them in the seat beside Aurora's. I considered claiming it, but her feet were touching mine, and she was only making casual conversation with the other guys. So, I remained where I was, and the chair was quickly filled with another male.

She greeted him, introducing herself and trying to remember his name. When their brief chat ended, she flashed me a brilliant smile that made me more certain I'd made the right decision.

Regardless of who she sat beside, she was mine.

That was what mattered.

An argument broke out across the room after the next round, and we all looked in time to watch one of our pack-mates throw a punch. The other caught a fist in his eye, before tackling the first to the ground and slamming his own fist into the first's face.

Aurora's eyes widened at the violence, and I brushed my foot against her leg. I was trying to let her know silently that she wasn't alone, and I wouldn't let anyone hurt her.

"Both of you are out," Ivaylo growled, as Ezra quickly crossed the room and uncovered two large hats. They were both cylindrical, and the tops of them were nearly exploding with the feather boas we were all wearing. They hung around it like odd, fuzzy chunks of hair.

Aurora covered her mouth to stop a laugh. We exchanged another set of grins, and her face remained slightly pink.

Thankfully, she didn't seem afraid after the fight.

And veil, I didn't think I'd ever seen her so *happy*.

I'd sit across from her every day, if it made her smile like that.

"You fought; now, you wear the hats of punishment," Ezra declared, carrying the massive, fuzzy things over to the guys.

Both took them without protest, wiping blood off their faces and setting the hats on their heads.

They looked even more ridiculous than I expected, and a few of the girls burst out laughing.

A few of the men followed, and I found my own grin widening at the humor on Aurora's face.

The game resumed soon enough, and we made it through two more rounds before my female was out.

She left her chair, and chatted with a few of the guys while I played through another two rounds. When I came out the victor, she walked over to me and draped her arms around my shoulders, leaning close.

My body relaxed with her presence, and the clear evidence to all of the men in the room that she considered herself mine as much as I did.

Her lips brushed my ear. "You didn't tell me you were so good at this game."

"I don't think you gave me the chance," I murmured back.

"Probably true. Mind if I sit with you until the next game starts?"

In response, I grabbed her waist and tugged her closer, making her laugh as she dropped onto my lap.

"Obviously, I picked the wrong teacher," she said playfully.

"Anyone could've told you that," Valko said, dropping into the chair next to mine. "The only one who can outplay Rok, is me."

Aurora shot him a curious look. "Have we met before?"

"You haven't. This is Valko, the other beta. Valko, this is Rory."

Understanding filled her eyes. "It's nice to meet you."

"Of course it is," Valko winked. "Now, you've met the attractive brother."

I elbowed him in the side, and he and Aurora both grinned.

"I didn't know you were brothers," she remarked.

"Not by blood," I explained. "But we've spent so much time holding the pack together, we may as well be family."

"Before our last alpha lost his battle with immis, the three of us were his betas," Valko added. "If he'd let us do our damn job, we wouldn't have lost so many wolves. We haven't lost anyone since Ivaylo took over."

"Knock on wood," Ezra said, plopping down next to Valko.

Valko and I frowned.

"It's a human saying. Like... don't count your eggs before they hatch," Aurora offered.

Our frowns deepened.

"They're telling you not to get cocky," Ivaylo said, scooping Ezra up and sitting beneath her smoothly.

"I don't think your cocks need any help, either," Ezra agreed, flashing her mate a wicked grin.

Aurora snorted, and the rest of us mirrored Ezra's expression.

"Did you win at your table?" Aurora checked, looking over at Ezra.

"Nah. Ivaylo wiped me out first." She rolled her eyes at him.

His grin widened. "You told me I wouldn't be able to."

"That was my way of telling you to let me win," she shot back, though she was grinning too.

He chuckled. "Where would be the fun in that?"

A few more of the chairs filled up, and one of the other guys passed out the cards.

"I hope you're all ready to lose," Valko announced, as the game began.

As expected, he may as well have cleaned the floors with us.

But damn, it was a good time anyway.

eighteen

RORY

MY FINGERS WERE LACED through Amarok's as the last of us finally funneled out of the pack's den.

Ezra and I had stayed to clean up with our mates after the party ended. We'd immediately been carried to the nearest couch and set down on our asses with heaping plates of food, but neither of us had protested.

We'd lost like champions, so it seemed fitting, anyway.

They'd finished cleaning soon enough, the guys chatting and tossing jokes back and forth. Honestly, the whole night had been so surreal to me, I couldn't stop myself from grinning.

Amarok and I weren't mated. Our relationship was about as far from stable as it could be in Evare's definition of the term, with no magic connecting us anymore. Yet, he had been calm. He had been level-headed. He had sat across from me without complaint, and hadn't been upset in the slightest when I smiled at and chatted with other men.

I'd made *friends*. Male friends, too. One of the other guys had even asked me if he could bring me food, and Amarok hadn't lost his shit or called me a slut or anything. He stood closer to me after I turned the guy down, but it wasn't a big deal at all.

Not because Amarok didn't care if someone else flirted with me, but because he was secure in our relationship. And honestly, I was too.

It was a good feeling.

A really, really good feeling.

I couldn't say I was ready to commit when there were so many things I didn't know about him, but it still felt good.

"Are we moving your stuff to my den tonight?" he asked me, our linked hands swinging a little between us as we made our way back.

I hesitated, and he waited patiently for me to answer.

Finally, I admitted, "I want to. I really, really want to. I'm just nervous about jumping all-in so soon. We still haven't known each other that long. Everything felt perfect with Allen at the beginning too, even though I can look back now and see the red flags."

"Then we'll wait." He said it like it was simple, like he wasn't frustrated, angry, or heart-broken. "There's no rush, Aurora. When we seal the bond, it'll tie us forever."

I nodded, relief relaxing my shoulders as we approached my den. "Thank you."

"What did I say about thanking me?" His voice was gruff, but playful too.

"Right, I need to think of something better." I went up on my tiptoes, and he bent down to kiss me. The kiss was soft and slow, and made me seriously reconsider going home alone.

But ultimately, I needed time to myself, to get reacquainted with my own mind.

So, I finally pulled away, smiled at him, said goodnight, and slipped into my den.

It felt much colder and emptier after two nights in Amarok's, but I sprawled out and let my mind go to the past.

A cold and empty bed was so damn much better than my life on Earth.

Casino Night had been fun, and eye-opening. I felt safer than ever with Amarok, even if I wasn't ready to commit entirely. He was willing to give me as much time as I needed before sealing our bond, and clearly had no intention of pushing me or rushing me into anything.

I'd managed to find everything I'd wanted and needed... and I'd done it in a magical world, of all places.

My lips curved upward, and I fell asleep happy.

Really, genuinely happy.

. . .

THE NEXT MORNING, we fell back into our routine. Amarok made me breakfast in his den, and we chatted over our food before spending the day working with the pack. We had lunch on our own and dinner in the pack's den, and parted ways at the entrance to my home.

Neither of us instigated sex. I wasn't sure if he wanted it—*I* definitely wanted it—but I wasn't sure how to go about suggesting it. Getting freaky in the kitchen didn't seem as natural as it had the night before the eclipse, so I didn't bring it up.

It was nice to talk, though. He told me stories about the creative ways they'd kept their packmates from losing their minds, and about how life had been before immis started setting in for anyone.

I told him stories about the happy parts of my childhood, and the good times I'd had before Allen took over my life.

I enjoyed it, but it didn't feel... honest.

It felt like we were dancing around the truth, though I wasn't entirely sure how, and I wasn't really ready to face that.

A week went by, and then another woman from Earth arrived on the back of another shifter guy. They weren't fated mates, so the single shifters swarmed her, parading her with gifts, flowers, and attention.

I worked with the other girls to keep them at bay and help her adjust, which cut my breakfasts with Amarok shorter than either of us wanted. Helping her seemed important, though, and he didn't protest, so I didn't think he minded too much.

A few more weeks passed quickly, and then there was another woman to welcome, and another, and another. I grew tired of going to sleep and waking up alone, but still didn't feel like I was ready to move to the next step with Amarok.

The next step would require commitment, and honestly, I was a little afraid of commitment.

So, I didn't say anything.

He didn't either.

My skin started to itch more and more as the need to shift grew stronger, but I knew there was a good chance I couldn't run without triggering another mate run for Amarok, so I stayed quiet about it.

And non-furry.

Very, very non-furry.

WHEN THE NEXT ECLIPSE APPROACHED,
it seemed to come out of nowhere.

I was eating lunch with a few of the girls when it clicked.

"You'll need to stay inside all day, if you don't choose one of the guys to spend it with," Riley explained to our newest human, letting her fingers brush almost absent-mindedly over her new, golden claim mark. The single women had been falling like flies, sealing bonds left and right. "And I would recommend not choosing a guy, unless you're pretty damn sure you want to mate with him."

"Shit. The eclipse is tomorrow, isn't it?" I asked them.

The girls all looked at me.

"Yes," one of the new ones confirmed.

"Where have you been?" Jill asked, lifting an eyebrow at me from where she stood in the kitchen. She even wore a golden claim mark.

"Not paying attention, apparently." I brushed my hair out of my eyes. "I need to go talk to Amarok. I'll be back in a few."

"You basically live here, Rory. Spend the day with your mate," Riley said, making a shooing motion.

I rolled my eyes at her, taking my empty plate to the sink. Jill plucked it from my hands and made the same motion Riley had, so, with a dramatic sigh, I headed out of the women's den.

My gaze scanned the land around us, searching for the furry black wolf. I didn't find him, which made me frown.

I hadn't had lunch with him in a few weeks... or months. But still, he usually waited for me.

Didn't he?

My chest tightened.

I debated walking back into the women's den and waiting to have the conversation with him at the end of the day.

But, I'd already told the girls I was leaving. And honestly, I wanted to know where he was.

So, I headed out to the den the men were excavating at the time. They'd filled in a bunch of older, empty ones a few decades earlier, so rather than digging new ones for the new women, they just cleared the old ones out and then fixed them up.

I scanned the working group, looking for Amarok. A few of the guys noticed and waved at me, and I waved back, but kept looking.

My lips curved down in a frown when I didn't find him.

Valko tossed his shovel to the ground and strode over to me. He'd gotten back with the newest woman, and was heading out again after the eclipse, I knew.

"Hey," I said, not bothering to adjust my frown. "Have you seen Amarok?"

"He left on a run a few hours ago. Usually heads south. Needed to get away, considering what today is." Valko gestured in that direction, his forehead creasing slightly as he studied me. "You know what today is, right?"

"I just realized," I said sheepishly, wrapping my arms around my abdomen. "We haven't talked about what we're going to do for the eclipse yet. I figured we should."

"I'm not talking about the eclipse, Rory."

My eyebrows wrinkled. "What are you talking about, then?"

Valko grimaced. "You'll have to ask him yourself. If he hasn't told you, there's probably a reason."

Hurt curled in my abdomen. "We don't really talk about the painful things. Is today an anniversary for something difficult?"

"Of course it is. Do you think life was easy here, for us?" He gestured toward the forest again. "There were thousands of single wolf shifters when Serae created her curse. We were down to *fifty* before she brought the first human here from your world. The guys we lost weren't strangers; they were our friends. Our families. Your life on Earth may have been shitty, but you're what, twenty years old? We've been here, losing the people we love, for centuries."

My throat swelled, and I whispered, "I didn't realize."

"Apparently." He shook his head, turned his back to me, and went back to his shovel.

Something told me he'd ended the conversation like that because if he didn't, he would've said something he might regret, and I'd never seen the shifters be purposefully cruel.

Tears stung my eyes as I slipped into the forest, heading south. I wanted to put myself somewhere that Amarok would catch my scent when he came back. Whatever bad had happened, I didn't want him to have to deal with it alone.

Finding a thick trunk, I sat down in front of it. The trees around me were still brown and green, so I was still on the pack's land.

I stared into the forest, forcing myself to consider everything Valko had said.

Amarok hadn't told me about anything painful in his past. He'd told me upbeat stories of how the guys kept each other alive.

But they didn't keep everyone alive.

They didn't even *almost* keep everyone alive.

They lost so many people... more than I could even imagine.

And he hadn't told me. Not the details, at least.

Because I hadn't been there for him.

He was there when I needed him, no matter what. If I was having a bad day, he'd pull me in for a hug. When I woke up sleepy, he made me a cup of the Evare version of coffee.

Every morning, I sat on the counter in his kitchen. He cooked me breakfast, and laughed and joked with me. He had realized I wasn't willing to take our relationship any deeper than it already was, and hadn't pushed me. He hadn't brought up anything negative, or asked me for anything more than I volunteered to give.

And I hadn't offered anything more than sharing the breakfast he cooked for us, and the day and two nights we'd shared during the last eclipse.

My throat swelled.

I had needed time to learn how to be free again… but he'd been alone during that.

The man was hurting, and I hadn't even realized. Not when he cooked for me, or when I cut our breakfast shorter than usual so I could check in with our newest human a little earlier. Not even when he brushed a kiss to my knuckles in goodbye and didn't linger outside the women's den after I stepped inside.

Amarok was a good man, and unlike me, a really, really good friend.

I wasn't willing to let him go, when he would either lose his fight with immis or pursue another woman. Both prospects were equally intolerable to me, for different reasons.

So, it was time for me to be his friend too.

I wasn't sure how well that would go over with him, after so many months of me putting in zero effort, but I'd figure it out.

I had also never pursued a man myself, so… yeah.

We'd see how it went.

nineteen

RORY

I WAITED FOR AN HOUR, trying to come up with ways to win him over, and hatched the beginning of a plan while I sat there. The sitting got old, though, and I wasn't sure how long I'd be waiting outside, which made me feel a little less certain about everything.

Another hour or so passed before I heard feet on the dirt behind me, and turned my head. I found Ezra padding toward me. Her long, bright red hair fell loosely over her shoulders and chest, and the huge, gray shirt she wore clearly belonged to Ivaylo.

"Hey, Valko told me you walked this way a while ago," she said, flashing me a quick smile as she covered the distance between us and plopped down on the dirt. "What's up?"

My throat swelled a little as my mind went back to my conversation with the beta. "Amarok is having a hard day, and I didn't realize."

She gave me a sad smile. "The guys have those sometimes."

I nodded, looking back out at the trees and blinking quickly. "I've been a shitty mate, and a shittier friend to him."

"In your defense, you didn't ask to be brought here." Ezra's shoulder bumped mine gently. "No one expected you to adjust quickly or easily, Rory."

"I love it here, though. This place saved me. Allen would've killed me eventually, if Serae hadn't gotten me out. And the transition might've been difficult if Amarok wasn't so good to me—or so determined to make it easy. But he made it simple, and never asked me for anything."

"He's a good guy."

"The best," I wrapped my arms around my knees, pulling them to my chest. "If you were going to seduce a werewolf, or convince him that you wanted to be with him, how would you do it?"

She laughed. "You don't really have to seduce a werewolf. They want you just because you exist."

My lips curved upward. "I know. But I've convinced him pretty thoroughly that I need to set the pace, and I think it's going to take more than words to make him realize that I don't want the relationship to stay one-sided."

"Hmm." She considered it. "Bringing him into your den would be a good first step, or moving into his. Having you in their space is really big for the guys."

I nodded.

I'd already figured out that much, and planned for it.

"Making desserts for him is another big one. The guys love taking care of us, but they want to be taken care of too, even if they won't admit it. The women in the other pack told me that in a traditional male/female shifter relationship, the man takes care of the woman's needs. The woman brings him the light and color he's been missing without her, by making treats, playing games, being spontaneous to balance out the guys' seriousness... stuff like that."

Hmm.

Amarok definitely wasn't spontaneous, by any definition of the word. Neither was I, truthfully.

But I could try.

And desserts, I could definitely handle. I cooked for the other human women fairly often, but never for him, because he'd never wanted me to.

Ezra finished with, "So, I guess if I was setting out to seduce a wolf shifter, I'd probably move my shit into his den and start baking desserts a lot. Without clothes on, as often as possible. I'd enthusiastically eat everything he cooked for me, too, and ask him to take me places under the guise of seeing more of his world, so we could spend more time together. I'd probably run with him in his wolf form a lot, too."

"Should I be concerned that you're planning how to woo another male, Ez?" Ivyalo rumbled.

Both of us jerked our heads as he stepped out beside the tree our backs were resting against. Despite his words, his lips were curved upward a little.

"Definitely. I desperately need *another* man following me into the forest every time I tell him to give me a few minutes. And to occupy me in bed—because you're not insatiable enough," she drawled.

I snorted.

Ivaylo's eyes gleamed wickedly. "That sounds like a challenge, mate."

"You think everything is a challenge," she tossed back, though she was grinning.

"Coming from your lips, it usually is." He bent down long enough to grab her by the waist and throw her over his shoulder. His eyes met mine for a moment. "Tell Rok I'm here if he needs to talk."

I nodded, my throat swelling again.

Whatever had happened must've been terrible.

I was going to do better at being there for him. So damn much better.

"Good luck, Rory!" Ezra called to me, as her mate hauled her back toward their den.

Standing up, I swept dirt off my ass.

I didn't know when Amarok was going to be back, but time by myself was exactly what I needed, for an entirely different reason, now.

IT DIDN'T TAKE TOO long to get back to my den and gather my stuff.

A few guys gave me curious looks when they saw me hauling things to Amarok's den over four different trips. One offered to help with the first batch. When I gave him a quick *no* and took a few hurried steps away from him, I think he got the message that I didn't want his scent anywhere near my shit.

Filling his den with stuff that smelled like me and another guy would lead to more issues, and we definitely didn't need more issues.

When I finally made it to the bottom of the ladder after my last trip, I looked out at the pile of my stuff I'd thrown in from above.

There was a lot of organizing to do.

I pulled the lever to lock the den—because I knew Amarok would be worried if he came back and learned that I left it open while I was home alone—and went to work.

Thankfully, most of what I owned was just clothes and toiletries. I'd left everything I didn't need, like my den's pillows and blankets, to avoid making a few more trips.

Humming a song whose lyrics I could only faintly remember, I started sorting and hanging my clothes. Amarok's only took up a small portion of the closet, so I made sure to spread mine out over the rest, to make it look as full as possible. Clothes disappeared into some kind of magical void when shifters shifted, so I'd stocked up on a lot of clothes after the dozenth time Riley and Jill warned me to do so, which meant I had a lot more than I needed.

But they filled the closet well, so I was glad.

When Amarok got back, he was going to be surprised by how *not alone* he was.

...Hopefully, pleasantly surprised.

I didn't like the thought that it might be an unpleasant surprise.

Not even a little.

So, I reminded myself that Ezra had the same idea I did about moving into the guy's den, and kept working.

I was the one who hadn't been there for him, so I was going to have to put in the time to change that, even if it was uncomfortable.

AMAROK STILL WASN'T BACK by the time I'd finished organizing my stuff, so I slipped out of my bodysuit and stepped into the kitchen in just my oversized shirt.

He had never told me what his favorite dessert was, but I knew the top three that most werewolf guys loved off the top of my head. I remembered Amarok eating a few of the caramel-like pastry things with a weird name, and found the recipe quickly enough, so I started on them. I'd watched him cook so often I knew where everything was, which made that easier.

The desserts were a lot more time-intensive than I expected, and required quite a bit of hand-kneading. The physical work eased the itch beneath my skin, so I didn't mind it at all.

My first pan was in the oven, with a timer set and the glaze ready to go, when there was finally a muffled knock on the thick stone lock keeping everyone else out. My eyes brightened, and I didn't bite back the smile that stretched across my face.

Though my hands were sticky with the dough that would become the second pan of his desserts, I hurried over to the lever and eased it open just a tiny bit. "Hello?"

"Aurora?" Amarok sounded cautious.

"Hey!" I forced myself to act a hell of a lot more confident than I felt, and tugged the lever the rest of the way open.

Though I wanted to hurry back to the kitchen and throw myself into baking again, I forced myself to wait while he jumped into the den, landing smoothly.

His eyes were a bit red, but neither of us mentioned it as they moved quickly over my body. He was making sure I was okay, though I didn't know why. "What happened? Did someone make you feel unsafe while I was gone?"

"What? No, of course not."

"Then what are you doing here?" His nostrils flared, and his gaze jerked to the kitchen. "Are those olinivs?"

"Yep!" I ignored his first question, giving him a quick hug before striding back toward my dough. My mind moved quickly, struggling to come up with a decent way to tell him that I had moved in.

His feet were silent, but I felt his attention leave me for a moment. When I peeked over my shoulder, I saw him glance at the bathroom before stepping into the doorway of the closet, and freezing.

My attention jerked back to the pastries, and I shoved my hands back into the dough, working on forming another ball into the strange shape I needed for them. Mine definitely didn't turn out as perfectly as the ones I'd seen at Casino Night, or the ones I'd watched Ezra make, but I hadn't been trained by the older shifter women like she had.

I felt his attention again, and a moment later, he was leaned up against the cabinets to my right. "Aurora?" His voice was low, and gruff. "Your clothes are in my closet."

I lifted my gaze to his, and gave him another quick smile. "Your offer to move in together still stands, right? We could always move to my den if you want, but nothing is as nice there, and I don't have a bathtub. Your tub is like something out of a dream, so I thought I—"

He cut me off by pulling me into a hug. A tight, fierce hug.

A soft, relieved breath escaped me as I wrapped my arms around him too. I hugged him back as tightly as I could without squashing the weird shape of my pastry dough against his back.

"Of course it stands," he said, his voice heavy with emotion.

"Good." I brushed my lips to his throat, and felt his cock harden quickly against my abdomen.

I wanted to ask him why he'd needed to leave and why his eyes were red like he'd been crying. But, I knew I couldn't push him to share whatever he'd been through. I needed to show him he could trust me with it, and give him time to want to tell me about it. "You know tomorrow is the eclipse, right?"

"I thought you'd want to spend it alone." He released me, and my throat swelled as I returned to my pastries.

"Why would I want to spend it alone?"

"You wanted time to adjust."

Right.

"I had enough time," I said simply.

When I glanced up at his eyes again, he didn't look convinced.

Not even a little.

"I didn't see your bedding," he said, instead of admitting that.

"I figured I didn't need it."

His chest rumbled unhappily. "Your scent is on it, Aurora."

"Alright, I'll go grab it after I finish the rest of these." I lifted the misshaped dough.

"I'll take care of it." He strode back to the ladder, and I squeezed my eyes shut as I heard him leave.

"Dammit," I whispered, dropping the pastry on the sheet and grabbing another chunk of dough.

I should've realized he wouldn't be thrilled to find me making myself at home in his den when he was having a shitty day. I should've known he wouldn't be comfortable coming to me with something difficult after I'd left so much space between us, too.

But... maybe I could fix that.

twenty

AMAROK

I DUCKED out from between the rocks over my den and let out a long breath.

I'd planned on spending the night and the next day alone in my den, after making sure Aurora was tucked away safely in her own space. I'd assumed I would have the time I needed to sit in my damn bathing pool and stare at the ceiling for a few hours, until my emotions were replaced by the eclipse's incessant lust.

Finding her in my den was highly unexpected.

Having her move in?

Even more so.

It wasn't an unpleasant revelation, of course. I had *wanted* her in my space for a long time.

It just caught me off guard, given the day and the state of my mind.

The eclipse would be far more enjoyable if we spent it together, but since I hadn't expected that either, it had also surprised me.

But she could worry if I wasn't back soon enough, so I forced my exhausted legs to carry me toward her den.

Valko fell into step beside me halfway there. "I talked to your mate earlier."

My head jerked toward him. "Did she tell *you* she was going to move in with me?" The words came out with more frustration than I expected.

Dammit, I was going to scare her back to her own space before the night was over. Moving the rest of her things was probably a waste of effort.

"No."

At least she hadn't confided in a different male.

I let out another long, rough breath.

"She doesn't know about Rov," Valko said.

My throat burned. "No."

"Or your parents?"

"Of course not."

He grabbed my arm as we reached her den—her *old* den—and looked me square in the eyes. "Why didn't you tell her, Rok?"

"She doesn't want to know." The words were low and angry. "She's worth fighting for, and waiting for, but she doesn't want to know."

He didn't look convinced. "She asked me what happened. You could be underestimating her."

"I'm giving her the space she needs. When she's had enough space, she'll tell me." I ran a hand through my hair, exhaustion dragging my shoulders down. "I need to get back to her. Good luck with the eclipse."

He dipped his head, stepping back and saying nothing as I dropped into the den my female had left open.

My chest rumbled as her scent engulfed me. Tilting my head back, I gave myself a moment to simply sit and breathe her in.

Veil, I ached for her.

Her thick scent eased my mind and relaxed my shoulders slightly as the moment I'd allowed myself passed. A few more followed, and I let my feet carry me to the edge of her bed.

Sitting down on the mattress, I closed my eyes and gave myself a few more minutes to wrap my mind around what had happened.

I'd spent the day reliving the past. When I got home, I followed her scent back to her den, then back to mine.

Her presence there caught me off guard, but that didn't mean it was a bad thing.

I wasn't sure what had changed to make her want to move in—and I clearly needed to ask her—but it was still good that she had.

Very, very good.

I could get used to coming home to the sight of my mate in my den.

Our den.

After a few more minutes, I gathered the rest of her things and headed home.

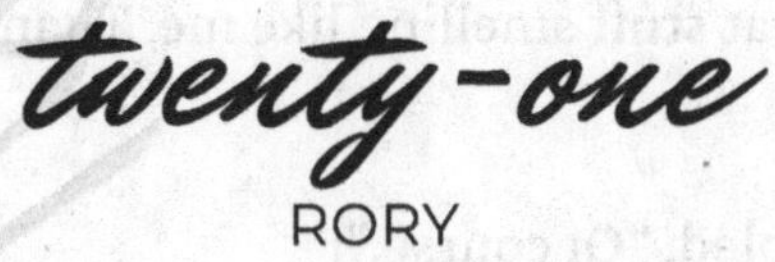

RORY

I MADE a mental list of possible ways to make Amarok's night better while I waited for him to come back. Clearly, the desserts hadn't been as much of a hit as I had hoped. It seemed like a miracle he hadn't dragged my ass back to my den and abandoned me there, so…

Yeah.

I'd messed up.

In multiple ways, as far as I could tell.

I wasn't used to needing to redeem myself, but I'd figure it out. I'd apologize, or fix it somehow.

Hopefully.

I was scrubbing the dishes while the first pan of my pastries cooled, when Amarok finally came back. He'd been gone so long, I almost worried he'd made a run for it.

I looked over my shoulder at him as he pulled the lever to lock us in, his arms full of my bedding.

When he caught me looking, he gave me a small smile.

That eased the fear in my chest, just a little. "Sorry, I didn't think about that stuff smelling like me. Thanks for grabbing it."

His chest rumbled. "Of course."

I turned back to my dishes, and he put my things away before joining me in the kitchen.

Rather than pulling my hands from the sink like I half-expected him to, he set his palms lightly on my waist.

My body flushed with the contact. I'd been at war with my lust for the man since the last damn eclipse, but hadn't let myself do anything about it.

"I'm sorry I didn't react well when I got back. You caught me off guard," he said quietly.

"It's alright. I should've asked you before just bringing my stuff over and making myself at home. I know a shifter's den is sacred to you guys."

"It's far more sacred with you in it, Aurora." He squeezed my hips lightly. "Are the olinivs for the new humans?"

"Oh, no. They're for you. A welcome home present, I guess. To ease the fact that I moved in without asking, maybe?" I bit my lip. "The shape is wrong, I know. And I think I was supposed to wait another minute before dunking them in the icing, so they're mushier than Ezra's, but—"

He let go of my hip with one hand, plucked a pastry off the drying rack, and took a bite. His chest rumbled with appreciation, and I relaxed more. "They don't need to look perfect to taste good. Thank you."

I nodded, and resumed washing the dishes.

He finished off the pastry before stepping back—and pulling me a few steps back with him. I stumbled a little, but his grip on my hips was steady enough to hold me upright.

When I opened my mouth to ask him why he'd moved me, he stepped between me and the sink, and took over doing the dishes.

A soft laugh escaped me. "Amarok."

"You can feed me another oliniv if you want to help."

A louder laugh escaped.

I lifted myself onto the counter and grabbed another pastry, lifting it to his lips. His expression was playful as he took a bite, still working on the dishes.

"It's not the end of the world if I clean up after myself," I said, giving him another bite.

"Of course it isn't. But I'm here, and you baked for me, so I'm going to clean up."

I shook my head at him, but couldn't fight the smile that curved my lips.

"What changed today?" he asked.

Neither of us needed clarification about what he was asking.

He wanted to know why I'd moved in so suddenly.

Maybe it would've been wiser to be vague, or give a half-answer, but I didn't want to do either of those things. I wanted to tell him the truth.

"I didn't realize the eclipse was tomorrow until lunch time," I admitted. "I went out to find you, to make sure we were on the same page about spending it together, but you were gone. I found Valko instead, and he told me how hard things were for you guys before we got here. I realized I'd been focused on the other humans, and myself, and haven't treated you as well as you deserve. So, I'm going to do better. Starting with this."

He blinked, his expression almost taken-aback.

"I know we're not mated right now, and we haven't really talked about our shitty pasts, but our relationship is permanent to me, too. Not because fate put us together, but because you've been here for me even when it's hard. You treat me well, even when I've given you no reason to. You're a good man, and I'm really, really glad it's you." I lifted my pastry back to his lips.

He didn't bite into it, this time.

Instead he stared at me, his eyes full of emotion.

Amarok finally shut off the water and took a small bite of the pastry. He dried his hands, then lifted me off the counter by my thighs. I wrapped my arms around his neck, the treat hanging down his back as I leaned against his chest.

"What are we doing?" I asked.

"Taking a bath. I've missed you."

I leaned closer. "I've been dreaming about having you naked again since the last time."

"I've been dreaming about a hell of a lot more than a little nudity."

My lips stretched in a smile.

He set me down on my feet, and I slipped my shirt over my head. His eyes moved slowly down my figure, his gaze hot. "Damn, Aurora."

"You're not so bad either," I teased him lightly, as he stepped out of his shorts.

A shriek escaped me as he grabbed me again and stepped into the tub in one fluid motion. The water quickly covered us to our shoulders, and I sighed as I relaxed against him. Neither of us made a move to do anything about his erection against my core, but his bare skin felt incredible on mine.

Amarok's arms wrapped around my back, pulling my chest tighter to his. He held me there, and I closed my eyes, relaxing in the silence. Some part of me I hadn't acknowledged in far too long seemed to calm under his touch, and peace eased my mind as we sat there together quietly.

A few moments passed before Amarok spoke again, his playfulness gone. "My brother died today."

My throat swelled.

"Not *today*, today. A long time ago, today. We were twins, and we spent damn near every minute together before. He was my best friend, but there wasn't anything I could do to convince him to keep fighting immis."

Tears welled in my eyes, too. "I'm so sorry."

"His name was Rov. Rov was..." Amarok gave a soft, low chuckle. "We were opposites. I was the quiet, steady one. He was the vibrant, fun one. We balanced each other out."

He admitted, "Immis was harder on the energetic guys. Those of us left are the stoics. We were the grittiest guys, the ones who knew how to cope when shit got hard. Keeping each other alive was always a challenge, but back when it first hit, we hadn't learned how to fight it. I didn't know how to help Rov, or how to convince him to hold out. It nearly killed me to lose him, but Valko and Ivaylo dragged me back from the ledge."

Tears rolled down my cheeks, leaking onto his shoulder and rolling down until they mingled with the water in the bathing pool. "I can't imagine how hard that must've been."

"I still miss him. I think I always will. But I try to find the fun in things, for him. I'm still shitty at it—probably always will be. But I try. Hopefully, that's enough."

I squeezed him tightly, needing him to know that I was there. That I was listening, and that I cared.

He hugged me back even tighter, and though we were bare, sex was the furthest thing from either of our minds.

"Will you tell me a story about him?" I whispered.

Amarok chuckled. "You'll probably run the other way if I do."

But he told me one.

And another.

And another.

Hours went by while we sat in the pool, talking about his brother and holding each other close. With every one that passed, I found myself holding Amarok tighter and tighter.

Because as much as I had tried to ignore my emotions, desires, and everything else as it applied to the werewolf, one thing became crystal clear:

I never wanted to hurt him again.

WE FINALLY DRIED off as our bodies began to warm with lust. Amarok had heard my stomach growl, so he carried me back to the kitchen and set me on the counter, whipping up food faster than I'd ever seen him cook before.

He cooked slowly in the mornings so we could spend more time together at breakfast, I realized.

It only made my body hotter.

After we ate together, we abandoned the plates on the table and moved back to the bed. He leaned his huge, warm body over mine and made love to me passionately, without any hurry.

The eclipse set in as we shattered together, and we were both lost to the heat of its lust again.

WHEN I WOKE up the morning after, Amarok was still snoring. My body was blissfully relaxed, and I cursed myself for ignoring what I wanted for so damn long after the last one had ended.

I wouldn't be making that mistake again.

My gaze lingered on Amarok's body for a few minutes before I slipped out from underneath his arm. After I used the facilities, I made my way to the kitchen and quietly began cleaning the dishes we'd left. He would've done it if I let him, but I didn't want him to have to wake up and clean.

I wanted him to wake up and see that I wasn't going anywhere. And to spend the day with me again, like he'd wanted to for far too long.

My lips curved upward as more of my plan formed in my mind.

I knew just how to seduce my werewolf... and exactly how to keep him forever.

. . .

I WAS FINISHING up the last of the dishes when the blankets rustled behind me.

Amarok's sleepy growl flooded the room, making me smile again. He'd be mad that I cleaned the dishes, but he would survive.

"Aurora," he grumbled, his feet nearly silent on the stone as he crossed the room.

"Good morning." I turned my head to kiss him as the front of his body met the back of mine. Though his eyes were narrowed, he kissed me without hesitation, his fingers sliding into my hair and deepening the kiss without pause.

I turned to kiss him back, angling my body. He lifted me onto the counter, and I didn't give a damn about my bare ass hanging over the ledge of the sink while he kissed me.

It did bug me when he pulled away. His grip was still tight in my hair as he said against my lips, "Why are you doing the dishes, Aurora?"

The fact that he was annoyed at me for cleaning up after both of us only made me even more sure that I was making the right choice.

"They're my dishes too, Amarok. I'm allowed to do them."

He captured my lips again, kissing me hard and fast. My fingers dug into his arms, holding him tight to me as his mouth made love to mine.

A few minutes later, he pulled away to growl at me again. "If you're up before me, wake me up."

"If I'm up before you, I'm going to do whatever the hell I want," I panted, resting my forehead against his. "Including the dishes."

"Aurora," he warned.

"I'm pretty sure your definition of punishment would include an orgasm or three, so go ahead and punish me," I whispered back.

His chest rumbled, and I couldn't tell whether it was with humor or frustration. Probably a bit of both. "I'm not joking, female. Let me take care of you."

Peeling my forehead off his, I lifted my hands to his face and cradled it between my hands. Our eyes met, our gazes steady. "If you get to take care of me, I get to take care of you too. Today, that includes me doing the dishes while you slept. Most days, I'll happily sit by and watch you clean. Got it?"

It was almost surreal to hear the command in my voice. It felt good to be confident that there would be no consequences for saying exactly what I felt to him, though.

No *bad* consequences, at least.

The tension in his shoulders eased slightly, and his gaze softened. "Got it." His lips brushed mine, and I kissed him again, slower and sweeter than before.

My legs hooked around his hips, and I used them to pull him closer. The length of his cock pressed against my clit, but neither of us moved to intensify the contact. His lips left mine again, and trailed slowly down my throat while one of his hands lifted to grip my breast.

"This is when you tell me how much you like waking up and finding me in your kitchen, naked," I breathed.

"I could've climaxed at the sight of your bare body moving in *our* kitchen the moment I opened my eyes," he said against my throat, following it down to my breasts.

My back arched as he caught one of my nipples in his mouth, his thumb brushing my clit.

My hips arched with the contact, and the head of his cock found my opening. With one more motion, I took him inside me.

He wasted no time, filling me hard and fast.

I gasped, my fingers digging into his hair. He worked my clit with his thumb and my nipple with his mouth. My hips rocked and my breathing grew shallow as he dragged me to the edge quickly.

When I finally detonated, he lost control with me, snarling and filling me with his release.

My forehead rested on his again as we both came down from the high of the pleasure.

"Damn, you're good," I whispered to him.

His chuckle rumbled my chest. "So are you."

"I'm not really doing much," I confessed.

"You're trusting me to take care of you. That's more than enough." His lips brushed mine in a quick kiss. "I need to start on breakfast. Do you have time to eat before we leave."

I frowned. "You have plans?"

He paused a beat, as if I'd caught him off guard with the question. "You're spending the day with the other humans, aren't you?" he finally asked.

Oh.

Right.

"Not today. They'll be fine without me."

He paused again, and I knew I'd surprised him once more.

"I was thinking we'd run today," I said carefully.

His cock throbbed inside me, *hard*. "Run?"

"Yes. I've been ignoring the itch for too long already."

A quiet growl escaped him. "You'll need to go with a few of the other women. Valko and Ivaylo will lock me in my den."

Amarok was still assuming I wanted space, and giving me more than I needed.

He was adorable.

So damn adorable.

And ridiculously sweet.

Apparently, I was going to have to spell it out for him, though.

"I'm going to run today, Amarok. And I want you to chase me."

His cock throbbed again, a few more times, and he hissed, "*Fuck.*"

A soft laugh escaped me. "From what I've heard, we'll do that, too."

"I need to feed you first."

"Probably a good idea," I agreed. "You want to wait a few minutes anyway in case I change my mind, right?" My voice was playful, and his lips curved in a grudging smile.

"Of course."

"I'm not going to change my mind, but I have no problem with waiting." After a moment's pause, I added, "As long as you're going to let me finish the dishes while you cook for us."

His chest rumbled, and he pulled out of me. "Only this time, Aurora."

"I'm not agreeing to that." I brushed my lips to his lightly, and he captured my mouth. The kiss was hot and needy, but he finally released me as he pulled out. My body ached at the loss of his hardness, but excitement was curled in my chest at what I knew was coming.

We would run together.

I would shift for the first time.

I was going to be a wolf... and Amarok was going to reignite the frenzy when he bit me.

And, when it felt right, I was going to bite him back.

When I did, there would be no more room for uncertainty. He would know that I was his, and he would be mine. And maybe we could figure out a way to heal from the shit in our pasts, together.

twenty-two

RORY

"I'LL MAKE US A TABLE TOMORROW," Amarok said, as we sat on the kitchen countertop together and ate the food he'd cooked. "Or tonight, if you want space when we get back from the run."

"I don't want you to keep giving me space," I reminded him. "I'm all in, now."

He didn't look convinced, but I knew it would take time for him to get there. I had waited too long and avoided him too much for him to have the kind of confidence in me that I wanted. "We can decide when we get there."

Yep, there was the uncertainty.

I did have an idea how to combat it, though...

"Some of the other women mentioned visiting spare dens when they wanted to get away," I remarked. "That could be fun. We could run for a while, and stop for the night somewhere completely new to me."

"You may not want to run that long after your first shift," he warned.

I tried not to take it personally that he'd basically shot down my idea.

It would take time for him to see that I was committed; I would prove it as the days went on. Until then, he wasn't doubting me. He was just trying to give me an out he thought I might want.

"Let's just decide while we're out there," I said.

Amarok dipped his head, and we both continued eating.

Maybe I needed to come up with even more ideas about how to convince him to believe me.

If I couldn't prove myself to him over the next few days, I decided I'd set another plan in motion.

With that settled, I focused on eating, and then took a quick shower to clean myself off when Amarok took our dishes, shooing me that way.

When I emerged a few minutes later, he was finishing up, and we headed out soon after.

I SLIPPED my fingers between Amarok's as we made our way off the pack's land. We passed a small group of unmated men, and I noticed Valko among them.

Valko lifted a hand in greeting as we passed, and Amarok raised his own hand in response.

I squeezed his hand lightly as we kept walking.

Neither of us spoke as the trees around us changed a bit, their shapes unique and interesting.

Finally, the black and red of the rest of the Woods broke through, and we stepped away from the last green tree.

"So, how do we do this?" I asked Amarok, looking over at him.

He lifted a shoulder. "What did the other women say about it?"

"Riley told me that if I ran, the instinct to shift would take over. That was about it."

He nodded. "Then I'd say you just run."

I gave him a dirty look. "That's not what I was asking about, and you know it."

His lips curved upward slightly. "When you run from me, the need to chase you will likely reignite my mate run. If it doesn't, I'll just follow you."

My eyebrows shot up. "There's a chance it won't start your mate run again?"

He nodded.

"What the hell? What if that happens?"

"It's unlikely."

My heart dropped into my stomach. He hadn't even offered an alternative idea for if his mate run didn't start again. "This was a bad idea."

"You can't ignore the itch forever, Aurora. You need to run; run."

I pressed my lips together.

It wasn't the running I was most excited about; it was being chased. Him biting me, and beginning our bond again, too.

"What if your mate run never starts again? Or what if it takes you to someone else the next time it ignites?" I tossed a hand toward the rest of the pack. "There aren't many women now, but in a few more months? A few more years? There will be plenty to choose from. I don't want to—"

His hands landed on my face, cutting me off. His eyes and voice were steady as he said, "We are fated, Aurora. Fate doesn't change its mind. I'm almost positive your run will trigger my frenzy, and if it doesn't, I will force my magic to restart the run as many times as it takes. I don't give a damn how long I have to wait before I claim you again; you are mine."

The certainty in his words relaxed me more than anything else could.

"Now, run for me." His lips brushed mine, the kiss soft and sweet.

Excitement slipped back in as I stepped away from him, turning so my back faced him. "Give me a head start, in case it takes a few minutes?" I called over my shoulder.

"Unless the frenzy takes control," he confirmed. "I won't be myself, if that happens. You'll see it in my eyes."

I could still remember the gold that had filled his dark irises the first day we met, so I was sure I would be able to tell if he wasn't in the driver's seat.

And even if he wasn't, I had seen enough on that day to know he wouldn't hurt me, regardless.

After one last, long breath, I ran.

The motions were uncertain at first, my feet slow and stumbling, but I quickly adjusted. The itch on my skin intensified as I moved, until finally, I lost control.

My body began to change, and I felt the ground give out beneath me before I crashed forward. My hands hit the dirt before my face could—but they weren't hands at all.

They were paws.

Furry, pink paws.

Holy shit, I really *was* a wolf.

I heard Amarok's howl behind me, and a shiver rolled down my spine.

It was a warning.

The frenzy was setting in, like he had expected.

He was coming for me.

I pushed myself harder, and moved faster than I had ever dreamed I would be capable of. Trees and bushes flew past me as I ran, their dark trunks and vibrant leaves contrasting powerfully as I sprinted. My lungs burned and my chest heaved with the effort, but still, I kept going.

My mate may not have said it aloud, but he wanted a chase, and I was going to do my damnedest to give him one.

I couldn't hear him behind me, but I knew that meant nothing. He was there; he was just a much better hunter than I was.

Weaving over massive rocks and around thick, dark bushes, I threw everything I had into the run...

Until a huge, dark wolf's side brushed mine just before he lunged in front of me.

I tried to stop myself, but failed miserably. My front paws scraped the dirt before my back ones lifted into the air, and my back slammed against his side.

My body shifted as soon as the pain registered, and thick, warm arms caught me before I could hit the ground.

Amarok righted me smoothly, his fingers digging into my bare hips as he stared me down with bright eyes that glowed gold. He walked me backward until my shoulder blades hit the smooth bark of a tree. "Mate."

"Hey," I breathed, my hands pressing against his chest. The frenzy's light blazed off his entire body, pulsing with the beat I could feel of his heart against my chest.

One of his hands lifted to my hair, sliding into the strands before tilting my head to the side.

His lips lowered to my throat, and brushed the skin once, then again, before—

I sucked in a breath at the sudden, sharp pain.

His tongue licked the wound a moment later, and the pain vanished quickly.

My chest rose and fell rapidly as the frenzy swelled around me, his magic immediately melding with my body again.

The gold in his eyes flared brighter as they met mine, and then his hips were easing away from mine.

A moment later, he had me turned around. My breasts and cheek met the tree at the same moment he slammed into me, making me gasp at the sudden fullness stretching me wider.

"Shit," I choked out, my fingers finding his hair and digging in deeply.

"You belong to me, female," his voice rumbled in my mind, his hips moving fast and smooth as he drove into me again and again.

Noises escaped me as I neared the edge—until his fingers found my clit.

Then, it was over too fast.

My cries echoed through the Woods as I found my pleasure, losing control around his cock. He roared with me, filling me with his release.

The glow around us faded as we both caught our breath, coming down from the high with our bodies still pressed together.

"Damn," I sighed, my cheek still pressed tightly to the tree.

Amarok's lips brushed the claim mark on my shoulder once, and then again, before he slid out of me.

Stickiness leaked down the insides of my thighs as he eased me away from the tree, still holding up most of my weight.

"That was fun." I turned my eyes a little to meet his, and found Amarok's lips curving upward.

"The most fun I've had in a long, long time."

"Want to do it again?"

He chuckled, the sound rich and happy. His shoulders were much more at ease than I'd seen them recently.

"First, I just want to run at your side." He kissed me lightly before murmuring against my lips, "Sound fair?"

"Extremely." I kissed him again, not ready to let go, before I finally ended it and stepped away from him. "Show me your forest, Amarok."

He shifted forms, and I did the same. It surprised me, how innate the motion was to me after being in that form only once, but I supposed it was a part of me.

I was a wolf.

And that seemed just as magical to me as anything else in Evare, if not more.

. . .

WE SPENT the rest of the day in the forest, weaving deeper and deeper into the Woods. It was more fun than I could ever remember having, as we chased each other and played in rivers and streams. At lunch time, we shifted back to eat a massive lunch of fresh fruit in a gorgeous, clear pond Amarok led me to.

I had never felt so content in my life.

As nighttime closed in on us, he asked if I wanted to head back to the pack's land or borrow one of the abandoned dens. I went with the second option, so we ran until he reached the den.

I heaved a sigh as we shifted back to our human forms, and his light, easy laughter floated through the trees. "We've been running all day, Aurora. You need to eat and sleep."

"I'm not that fragile. Sometimes, you take care of me a little too much," I countered, as I stumbled into his arms.

Maybe I was more tired than I'd admitted to myself.

He held me against his side, his lips stretched in a wide grin as he led me into the massive trunk of a tree. When we were inside, he scooped me into his arms and jumped into a pit that I knew was the entrance to the den.

It was about the same size as ours, though there were sheets over what little furniture there was inside it.

"The bedding will be in the closet," he told me, walking me toward the bed.

"I'll grab it while you pull the sheets off," I said.

For once, he agreed to let me help. His lips brushed my forehead, and he released me so we could get to work setting up the room.

twenty-three

RORY

SOON ENOUGH, we were snuggled up together in the bed with our backs to the wall, eating a dinner of fruit he'd collected from a bush nearby. The den smelled a bit strange, which I didn't love, but we'd spent so much time running that our fur wasn't itching yet.

Our legs were tangled, and one of his hands held one of mine, his fingers intertwined with my own.

"Damn, this was a good day," I sighed, my voice thick with a happy sort of exhaustion.

"It was." Amarok brushed a kiss to the top of my head.

We finished eating, then crashed in each other's arms, a little sticky from the fruit but not giving a damn about it.

. . . .

MY STOMACH WAS GROWLING AGAIN

when I woke up, and Amarok was sleepily reaching for the last few fruits we hadn't eaten the night before.

"Sorry," he murmured, putting a fruit in my hand and then patting my hair lightly before he dropped his back to the mattress. A low, content sigh escaped him when he was sprawled out again, and my lips curved upward.

His hand started moving slowly over my thigh while I ate, the frenzy's glow growing brighter as he continued to touch me. Though my body was warm and I was wet with desire, neither of us made a move to sexualize the moment.

It was too damn intimate.

"It feels good to be away from the pack," I said, as I relaxed against his arm.

"It does." He continued stroking my leg. "Will you tell me about Allen?"

I sighed. "It'll ruin the peace."

"He doesn't have that power over you anymore. The peace will remain." He squeezed my thigh lightly.

Honestly?

I believed him.

Hell, I *agreed* with him.

Allen had no control over me anymore, and he never would.

"What if it changes how you feel about me?" I asked him, quietly.

"That's an impossibility."

I made a noise of disagreement.

"If it changes how I feel about you, you can sit on my cock until my feelings change back."

A snort escaped me, and he chuckled, starting to stroke my leg again.

My smile faded as I stared up at the ceiling, growing contemplative.

Did I trust Amarok not to look at me differently after he understood everything I'd been through? He had seen the bruises, so he knew that aspect of it, at least. And I didn't think the other stuff would really affect how he felt about me.

But... did I want him to know everything?

I thought back to the way he'd held me while he told me about his brother.

To the hours we'd spent discussing it, because he needed someone to talk to about it and wanted me to know.

I wasn't sure I wanted to talk to *anyone* about everything Allen had done to me... but, I did think it would free me from him even more when the past was no longer a secret.

And ultimately, I couldn't leave anything between me and Amarok. Not if I wanted our relationship to be a safe one, where we could both trust each other.

So, I took a deep breath, and started from the beginning.

Though his body moved closer and his free hand caught mine, he continued stroking my leg lightly, making sure I was comfortable.

Making sure I knew he wasn't judging me, and that his feelings for me weren't changing.

Even when his grip on my hand grew tight and his chest rumbled unhappily, he kept touching me.

And honestly?

It meant everything to me.

When I finally finished the story of meeting Serae on that bench and then meeting him, Amarok pulled me into his arms and hugged me. His grip was fierce, but not painful. Never painful.

The man knew how not to trigger me, and he had since the moment he saw those bruises on my face when we met. He didn't treat me like I was fragile, but like I was important. He just wanted me safe and happy; there wasn't anything else he had ever pushed me for.

And I wanted him safe and happy too.

Hell, I wanted more than that.

I wanted him to be safe, happy, and *mine*.

Permanently.

I had seen the mated men; they doted on their women just as much as the unmated ones, if not more. Their personalities and effort didn't change after they had claimed their woman permanently.

So, what was I waiting for?

I lifted my mouth to Amarok's, and kissed him.

I kissed him softly.

Sweetly.

And passionately, when his hands found my ass and gripped me tightly, rolling onto his back so I was in control.

Amarok didn't think I was broken after everything I'd been through.

He thought I was *strong*.

Our mouths made love as our bare bodies pressed against each other, and he tilted my hips slightly. Just enough that he found my entrance, so that when I lowered my ass, the head of his cock slid inside me.

Our breathing picked up together, the frenzy glowing brightly around us as we kissed until we couldn't any longer, releasing each other's mouths so we could breathe while we moved.

He thrust from below me while I rolled my hips, my cries of pleasure filling the air when he hit me in all the right places.

Every damn one of them.

I wanted to sit up, but my teeth were lengthening in my mouth, growing sharper.

I wanted him more.

I wanted *us* more.

So I leaned down and kissed his throat, like he had mine.

His body went still as his cock throbbed inside me.

I didn't make him wait any longer.

My teeth cut through his skin, and the taste of his blood flooded my mouth. It was tangy but sweet, tasting the way our den smelled.

Like him.

Like *home*.

"Veil, Aurora," he snarled, slamming into me as he lost control. His pleasure and movements drove me over the edge, and I released his throat as I cried out with my own climax, riding him with every damn ounce of energy I had left.

Both of us breathed hard as we came down from the high. The glow of our frenzy disappeared entirely, and my hands spread over the ridged muscles on his abdomen. My gaze was glued to his neck.

I watched the bite mark I'd left slowly heal, and then shimmer gold.

Gold, because our bond was sealed.

When I lifted my eyes to Amarok's, I found them focused on my neck, even more intently than mine had been on his. The emotions in his gaze were brilliant, and breathtaking.

He was brilliant and breathtaking.

"Thank you, Aurora," he finally said, lifting those emotion-filled orbs to my own. "I love you. Veil, I love you more than I could ever describe."

Tears stung my eyes. "I love you, too."

He pulled my mouth back down to his and kissed me, slowly and searingly.

And then he rolled me over and made love to me again, slower.

Sweeter, too.

When his voice repeated in my mind as he drove into me, *"I love you,"* I sent the words right back. *"I love you too."*

For the first time I could remember, I hoped nothing would ever change.

I hadn't needed a black-market identity after all; I'd just needed a fresh start in an entirely different world.

And the universe had delivered that, and so much more.

WE STAYED out in the Woods for a few days, running, making love, and gorging ourselves on fruit. The borrowed den had a bathtub Aurora liked almost as much as she liked ours, so we spent a decent amount of time in there, too.

After a week had gone by, we got company.

Uninvited company, but company nonetheless.

"It's a good thing you guys leave clothes everywhere," Aurora whispered, tugging a massive shirt over her bare body and making a half-hearted attempt to fix her hair.

It was unfixable.

I'd messed it up far too much while I made love to her against one of the walls an hour earlier.

"I'm sure it's just some of the guys checking to make sure we're both alive," I said, smoothing her hair like I thought it would help.

It wouldn't, but she didn't need to know that.

And honestly, I just wanted to touch her.

She nodded, and I tugged the lever to open the thick sheet of stone covering our doorway.

"Hello?" Ezra called down from above us.

I grumbled, and Aurora slipped her hand through my arm. Her grip eased my mood, and I couldn't stop myself from brushing a kiss to the top of her head.

"Hey," Aurora called back. "Is everything okay? We're fine out here, just honeymooning."

"You're mated?" Ezra demanded.

"Yep!"

A few whoops and cheers erupted outside, and my lips curved upward slightly.

Our female alpha definitely hadn't come alone.

"Well, congrats! Sorry to ruin the mood, but Serae just dropped off a human who's about to pop."

There was a pause.

"About to pop, as in..." Aurora trailed off, her eyes wide.

"Yeah. Very, very pregnant, with a little human."

"Shit. I'm coming." She surged toward the ladder, and I stopped her just long enough to kiss her. She pulled away soon enough, flashing me a grin before calling back, "*We're* coming.

My hands brushed her hips as I helped her up the ladder, knowing she wanted to climb up there herself. When we surfaced, I watched her throw her arms around Ezra, and give the handful of guys with her a quick smile.

Then, she stepped back to my side.

My chest burned with pride.

My female loved me, and trusted me.

I slid a hand around her waist, setting it lightly on her hip. I still didn't want to push her *too* much.

"You know you can touch me and kiss me whenever you want, now," she remarked, flashing me another grin.

The burning in my chest grew hotter.

It was a damn good thing our frenzy was over, or I would've needed to take her behind a tree and make love to her just for that damn remark.

"A baby, huh?" Aurora asked Ezra.

She grinned. "Yep. Looks like our pack's about to change again."

Aurora mirrored her grin. "I'm looking forward to it."

We all shifted together, and my mate's side brushed mine.

As it did, I couldn't help but realize the truth:

I was finally looking forward to the future, too.

epilogue

AMAROK—MANY YEARS LATER

"STOP FEEDING ME," Aurora complained, nestled in close to my side in the corner of the pack's den.

I couldn't help my grin.

My mate had become the pack's doctor as more of the mated females started having pups, but considering she was going to have our baby in the next few weeks, I had insisted she take the day off.

My definition of that involved her eating a lot.

Hers involved running. A lot of running.

We'd settled the debated by deciding that she would eat, then we would run, and finally, we would eat more.

We were on the third step of that plan, and she was refusing to take the last two bites of the last olinov I was feeding her.

"I swear, I'm going to puke if I take another bite," she sighed, leaning against me. "This baby needs to be evicted, pronto."

"She'll come out when she's ready." I brushed a kiss to her forehead.

"I know. I just wanted her to be ready last week."

I played with her hair as we watched a group of pups run around the den. The center of it had been cleared out for the most part, with climbing toys placed strategically around the space.

"They're so adorable," she said, her gaze following the little girls. "I can't believe we're going to be parents."

"Neither can I."

"Have you thought about names?"

I made a noncommittal noise. "I'm not picky."

"I've been thinking..." She bit her lip.

"Tell me." I tugged her hair lightly, and her lips curved upward in a small smile.

"We could call her Arovva. After your brother. Valko's mom was telling me that it's a popular name among shifter women, and I thought she would like to have a connection to them too, since we don't have any blood family."

Emotion swelled in my chest. Pride and love, warring. "I would love that."

She smiled, lifting her lips to mine and kissing me lightly. "It's settled, then."

I murmured my agreement, lifting her onto my lap. She laughed, leaning her head back against me as she settled into place. "I love you, Amarok."

"I love you too."

Fuck, I was glad I had fought Immis as long as I had. Having her in my arms was worth every damn moment of pain I suffered.

afterthoughts

Every time I write a book, I have a different idea or concept. Sometimes, it's a quote I like that I want to match the vibes of. Other times, I've already written the blurb and am just trying to tell the story that matches it (spoiler: this method has yet to work well).

For this one, the concept was one sentence. I had been reading a lot of books with dominant men (which are sexy, obviously) but maybe a little TOO dominant. There's a fine line between dominance and cruelty, one I am very particular about.

So, I wanted to high-tail it to the opposite of dominance, to see what would happen. I still wanted that sexy confidence, but to a quieter, calmer level, and this is what I came up with.

I quote my own plan here, very eloquently:

She says no, he says okay.

Quite the masterpiece, isn't it?

Hahahaha.

Anyway, that was the whole concept. I wanted to put a
woman who *needed* freedom for a valid reason, with a man
who was willing to give her space and time to heal without
being in her face.
Do I like in-your-face guys?
If you've ready many of my books, you probably know that I
do, very much.
But I wanted to see Rory develop confidence in herself *before*
she sealed herself to Amarok. If she was going to be with
him, it had to be because she wanted to and trusted him,
not because it was what had to happen.
Was it an easy story to write?
It certainly was not.
Did it go exactly how I expected?
Of course not.
It never does!
But to me, this story was beautiful in a gentle way because
of that soft, slow love. Nothing is ever perfect, but that's
what makes it real, I think.
As always, thank you so much for reading!
All the love,
Lola Glass <3

stay in touch

If you want to receive Lola's newsletter for new releases (no spam!) use this link:

<u>LINK</u>

Or find her on:
FACEBOOK
TIKTOK
INSTAGRAM
PINTEREST
GOODREADS

all series by lola glass

Standalones:

Deceit and Devotion

Claimed by the Wolf

Forbidden Mates

Wild Hunt

Kings of Disaster

Night's Curse

Outcast Pack

Feral Pack

Mate Hunt

Series:

Burning Kingdom

Sacrificed to the Fae King

Shifter Queen

Wolfsbane

Shifter City

Supernatural Underworld

Moon of the Monsters

Rejected Mate Refuge

about the author

Lola is a book-lover with a *slight* romance obsession and a passion for love—real love. Not the flowers-and-chocolates kind of love, but the kind where two people build a relationship strong enough to last. That's the kind of relationship she loves to read about, and the kind she tries to portray in her books.

Even though they're fun stories about sassy women and huge, growly magical men ;)

www.ingramcontent.com/pod-product-compliance
Lightning Source LLC
Chambersburg PA
CBHW012025110726
47995CB00005B/1124